Books by

JUNICHIRO TANIZAKI

THE KEY

THE MAKIOKA SISTERS

*Unesco Collection of Representative Works:
Japanese Series*

SOME PREFER NETTLES

The Key

[handwritten inscription] Ulegundo

Osaka '93

The Key

Junichiro Tanizaki

Translated from the Japanese by

HOWARD HIBBETT

CHARLES E. TUTTLE COMPANY
Suido 1-chome, 2-6, Bunkyo-ku, Tokyo

Originally published in Japanese as *Kagi*

Published by the Charles E. Tuttle Company, Inc., of Rutland, Vermont and Tokyo, Japan, with editorial offices at Suido 1-chome, 2-6, Bunkyo-ku, Tokyo, Japan, by special arrangement with Alfred A. Knopf, Inc., New York.

First Tuttle edition published 1971
Eighth printing, 1991

PRINTED IN JAPAN

The Key

NEW YEAR'S DAY

•

This year I intend to begin writing freely about a topic which, in the past, I have hesitated even to mention here. I have always avoided commenting on my sexual relations with Ikuko, for fear that she might surreptitiously read my diary and be offended. I dare say she knows exactly where to find it. But I have decided not to worry about that any more. Of course, her old-fashioned Kyoto upbringing has left her with a good deal of antiquated morality; indeed, she rather prides herself on it. It seems unlikely that she would dip

3

into her husband's private writings. However, that is not altogether out of the question. If now, for the first time, my diary becomes chiefly concerned with our sexual life, will she be able to resist the temptation? By nature she is furtive, fond of secrets, constantly holding back and pretending ignorance; worst of all, she regards that as feminine modesty. Even though I have several hiding places for the key to the locked drawer where I keep this book, such a woman may well have searched out all of them. For that matter, you could easily buy a duplicate of the key.

I have just said I've decided not to worry, but perhaps I really stopped worrying long ago. Secretly, I may have accepted, even hoped, that she was reading it. Then why do I lock the drawer and hide the key? Possibly to satisfy her weakness for spying. Besides, if I leave it where she is likely to see it, she may think: "This was written for my benefit," and not be willing to trust what I say. She may even think: "His real diary is somewhere else."

Ikuko, my beloved wife! I don't know whether or not you will read this. There is no use asking, since you would surely say that you don't do such things. But if you *should*, please believe

4

that this is no fabrication, that every word of it is sincere. I won't insist any further—that would seem all the more suspicious. The diary itself will bear witness to its own truth.

Naturally I won't confine myself to things she would like to hear. I must not avoid matters that she will find unpleasant, even painful. The reason why I have felt obliged to write about these things is her extreme reticence—her "refinement," her "femininity," the so-called modesty that makes her ashamed to discuss anything of an intimate nature with me, or to listen on the rare occasions when I try to tell a risqué story. Even now, after more than twenty years of marriage, with a daughter herself old enough to marry, she refuses to do more than perform the act in silence. Never to whisper a few soft, loving words as we lie in each other's arms—is that a real marriage? I am writing out of frustration at never having a chance to talk to her about our sexual problems. From now on, whether she reads this or not, I shall assume that she does, and that I am talking to her indirectly.

Above all, I want to say that I love her. I have said this often enough before, and it is true, as I think she realizes. Only, my physical stamina is no match for hers. This year I will be fifty-five (she must be forty-four), not a particularly decrepit age, yet somehow I find myself easily fatigued by love-making. Once a week—once in ten days—is about right for me. Being outspoken on a subject like this is what she most dislikes; but the fact is, in spite of her weak heart and rather frail health she is abnormally vigorous in bed.

This is the one thing that is too much for me, that has me quite at a loss. I know that I am inadequate as a husband, and yet—suppose she became involved with another man. (She will be shocked at the very suggestion, and accuse me of calling her immoral. But I am only saying "suppose.") That would be more than I could bear. It makes me jealous even to imagine such a thing. But really, out of consideration for her own health, shouldn't she make some attempt to curb her excessive appetites?

What bothers me most is that my energy is steadily declining. Lately, sexual intercourse leaves me exhausted. All the rest of the day I am too worn out to think. . . . Still, if I were asked whether I dislike it, I would have to say no, quite the opposite. My response to her is by no means

6

reluctant; I never have to whip up my desire out of a sense of duty. For better or worse, I am passionately in love with her. And here I must make a disclosure that she will find abhorrent. I must tell her that she possesses a certain natural gift, of which she is completely unaware. Had I lacked experience with many other women I might have failed to recognize it. But I have been accustomed to such pleasure since my youth, and I know that her physical endowment for it is equaled by very few women. If she had been sold to one of those elegant brothels in the old Shimabara quarter, she would have been a sensation, a great celebrity; all the rakes in town would have clustered around her. (Perhaps I shouldn't mention this. At the very least, it may put me at a disadvantage. But will knowing about it please her, or make her feel ashamed, or perhaps insulted? Isn't she likely to feign anger, while secretly feeling proud?) The mere thought of that gift of hers arouses my jealousy. If by any chance another man knew of it, and knew that I am an unworthy partner, what would happen?

Thoughts of that kind disturb me, increase my sense of guilt toward her, till the feeling of self-reproach becomes intolerable. Then I do all

I can to be more ardent. I ask her to kiss my eyelids, for example, since I am peculiarly sensitive to stimulation there. For my part, I do anything she seems to like—kiss her under the arms, or whatever—in order to stimulate her, and thus excite myself even more. But she doesn't respond. She stubbornly resists these "unnatural games," as if they had no place in conventional love-making. Although I try to explain that there is nothing wrong with this sort of foreplay, she clings to her "feminine modesty" and refuses to yield.

Moreover, she knows that I am something of a foot-fetishist, and that I admire her extraordinarily shapely feet—one can hardly think of them as belonging to a middle-aged woman. Still—or therefore—she seldom lets me see them. Even in the heat of summer she won't leave them bare. If I want to kiss her instep, she says "How filthy!" or "You shouldn't touch a place like that!" All in all, I find it harder than ever to deal with her.

To start off the New Year by recording my grievances seems rather petty of me, but I think it is best to put these things in writing. Tomorrow will be the "First Auspicious Night." Doubtless she will want us to be orthodox, to follow the

8

time-honored custom. She will insist on a solemn observance of the annual rite.

JANUARY 4

• •

Today an odd thing happened. I've been neglecting my husband's study lately, and went to clean it this afternoon while he was out for a walk. And there on the floor, just in front of the bookshelf where I'd put a vase of daffodils, lay the key. Maybe it was only an accident. Yet I can't believe he dropped it out of sheer carelessness. That would be very unlike him. In all his years of keeping a diary he's never done anything of the kind.

Of course I've known about his diary for a long time. He locks it in the drawer of the writing table and hides the key somewhere among the books or under the carpet. But that's all I know, I don't care to know any more than that. I'd never dream of touching it. What hurts me, though, is that he's so suspicious. Apparently he doesn't feel

9

safe unless he takes the trouble to lock it away and hide the key.

But then, why should he have dropped the key in a place like that? Has he changed his mind and decided he wants me to read it? Perhaps he realizes I'd refuse if he asked me to, so he's telling me: "You can read it in private—here's the key." Does that mean he thinks I haven't found it? No, isn't he saying, rather: "From now on I acknowledge that you're reading it, but I'll keep on pretending you're not"?

Well, never mind. Whatever he thinks, I shall never read it. I haven't the faintest desire to penetrate his psychology, beyond the limits I've set for myself. I don't like to let others know what is in my own mind, and I don't care to pry into theirs. Besides, if he wants to show it to me I can hardly believe what it says. I don't suppose reading it would be entirely pleasant for me, either.

My husband may write and think what he pleases, and I'll do the same. This year I'm beginning a diary of my own. Someone like me, someone who doesn't open her heart to others, needs to talk to herself, at least. But I won't make the mistake of letting him suspect what I'm up to.

I've decided to wait until he goes out before I write, and to hide the book in a certain place that he'll never think of. In fact, one reason why keeping a diary appeals to me is that although I know exactly where to find his, he won't even realize I have one. That gives me a delicious sense of superiority.

Night before last we observed the old New Year's custom—but how shameful to put such a thing in writing! "Be true to your conscience," my father used to say. How he would grieve at the way I've been corrupted, if he only knew! . . . As usual, my husband seemed to have reached an ecstatic climax; as usual, I was left unsatisfied. I felt miserable afterward. He's always apologizing for his inadequacy, yet attacks me for being cold. What he means by cold is that, to put it his way, I'm far too "conventional," too "inhibited"—in short, too dull. At the same time, I'm "splendidly oversexed," he says, quite abnormally so; it's the one thing I'm not passive and reserved about. But he complains that for twenty years I've never been willing to deviate from the same method, the same position. And yet my unspoken advances never escape him; he's sensitive to the slightest hint, and knows immediately what I want. Maybe it's because he's afraid of my too-frequent demands.

He thinks I'm matter-of-fact and unromantic. "You don't love me half as much as I love you," he says. "You consider me a necessity, a defective one at that. If you really love me you ought to be more passionate. You ought to agree to anything I ask." According to him, it's partly my fault that he's not able to satisfy me fully. If I'd try to stir him up a bit he wouldn't be so inadequate. He says I won't make the slightest effort to co-operate with him—as hungry as I am, all I do is sit back calmly and wait to be served. He calls me a cold-blooded, spiteful female.

I suppose it's not unreasonable of him to think of me in that way. But my parents brought me up to believe that a woman ought to be quiet and demure, certainly never aggressive toward a man. It's not that I lack passion; in a woman of my temperament the passion lies deep within, too deep to erupt. The instant I try to force it out, it begins to fade. My husband can't seem to understand that mine is a pale, secret flame, not one that flares up brilliantly.

I've begun to think our marriage was a dreadful mistake. There must have been a better partner for me, and for him too; we simply can't agree in our sexual tastes. I married him because my parents wanted me to, and for all these years I've thought marriage was supposed to be like this. But now I have the feeling that I accepted a man who is utterly wrong for me. Of course I have to put up with him, since he's my lawful husband. Sometimes, though, the very sight of him makes me queasy. Yes, and that feeling isn't new. I had it the first night of our marriage, that long-ago honeymoon night when I first went to bed with him. I still remember how I winced when I saw his face after he'd taken off those thick-lensed glasses of his. People who wear glasses always look a little strange without them, but my husband's face seemed suddenly ashen, like a dead man's. Then he leaned down close, and I felt his eyes boring into me. I couldn't help staring back, blinking, and the moment I saw that smooth, slippery, waxy skin I winced again. Though I hadn't noticed it in the daytime, I could see a faint growth of beard under his nose and around his lips—he's inclined to be hairy—and that too made me feel vaguely ill.

Maybe it was because I'd never seen a man's

face at such close range before, but even now I can't look at him that way for long without feeling the same revulsion. I turn off the bed lamp to avoid seeing him, but that's precisely when he wants it on. And then he wants to pore over my body, as minutely as possible. (I try to refuse him, but he's so persistent about my feet, in particular, that I have to let him look at them.) I've never been intimate with another man—I wonder if they all have such disgusting habits. Are those gross, sticky, nasty caresses what you have to expect from *all* men?

JANUARY 7

•

Today Kimura paid us a New Year's call. I had just started reading Faulkner's *Sanctuary*, and went back up to my study as soon as we had exchanged our greetings. He talked with my wife and Toshiko in the sitting room for a while, then, around three o'clock, took them out to the movies. He came back with them at six, stayed for dinner, and left after chatting till about nine.

14

At mealtime everyone except Toshiko had some brandy. Ikuko seems to be drinking a little more these days. I'm the one who initiated her, but from the first she has had a taste for it. If you urge her, she will drink a fair amount. It's true that she feels the effects of it, but in a sly, secret way, not letting it show. She suppresses her reaction so well that people often don't realize how much she's had. Tonight Kimura gave her several sherry glasses full. She turned a little pale, but didn't seem intoxicated. It was Kimura and I who became flushed. He doesn't hold his liquor very well—not as well as Ikuko, in fact. But wasn't tonight the first time she let another man persuade her to have a drink? He had offered one to Toshiko, who refused and said: "Give it to Mama."

For some time I have felt that Toshiko keeps aloof from Kimura. Is it because she thinks he is too attentive to her mother? That notion had also occurred to me; but I decided that I was being jealous, and tried to dismiss it. Perhaps I was right after all. Though my wife is usually cool toward guests, especially men, she is friendly enough to Kimura. None of us has mentioned it, but he rather resembles a certain American film actor—

who seems to be her favorite. (I've noticed that she makes a point of seeing all his films.)

Of course I've had Kimura visit us often, because I consider him a possible match for Toshiko; and I've asked my wife to see how they get along together. However, Toshiko doesn't seem at all interested in him. She does her best to avoid being alone with him; whenever he comes to see her, even when they go out to the movies, she invariably asks her mother to join them.

"You spoil everything by trailing along," I tell Ikuko. "Let them go alone." But she disagrees, and says that as a mother it's her responsibility to accompany them. When I reply that her way of thinking is outmoded, that she ought to trust them, she admits I'm right—but says that Toshiko wants her along. Supposing she does, isn't it because she knows her mother likes him? Somehow I cannot help feeling that they have a tacit agreement about this. Although Ikuko may be unaware of it—may believe that she is merely acting as a chaperone—I think she finds Kimura extremely attractive.

••

Last night I was a little intoxicated, but my husband was worse. He kept after me to kiss his eyes, something he hasn't insisted on lately. And I'd had just enough brandy to do it. That would have been all right, except that I happened to look at the one thing I can't bear—his gray, lifeless face after he's taken off those glasses. When I kiss him I close my eyes, but last night I opened them before I finished. His waxy skin loomed up before me like a wide-screen close-up. I winced. I felt my own face go pale. Luckily, he soon put his glasses back on, as usual to begin poring over me. I said nothing, and turned off the bed lamp. He stretched out his hand, trying to find the switch, but I pushed the lamp away. "Wait a minute!" he begged. "Let me have another look. Please . . ." He groped in the dark, but couldn't find the lamp, and at last gave up. . . . An unusually long embrace.

I violently dislike my husband, and just as violently love him. No matter how much he disgusts me I shall never give myself to another man. I couldn't possibly abandon my principles of right and wrong. Although I'm driven to my wit's end by his unhealthy, repulsive way of love-making, I can see he's still infatuated with me, and I feel that somehow I have to return his love.

If only he had more of his old vigor . . . Why has his vitality drained away? To listen to him, it's all my fault: I'm too demanding. Women can tolerate it, he says, but not men who work with their intellect: that kind of excess soon tells on them. He embarrasses me with such talk, but surely he knows I'm not to blame for my bodily needs. If he really loves me he ought to learn how to satisfy me. Yet I do hope he'll remember that I can't stand those revolting habits of his. Far from stimulating me, they spoil my mood. It's my nature to cling forever to the old customs, to want to perform the act blindly, in silence, buried beneath thick quilts in a dark, secluded bedroom. It's a terrible misfortune for a married couple's tastes to conflict so bitterly on this point. Is there no way we can come to an understanding?

•

Kimura came over at about half-past four today, to bring us some mullet roe that his parents in Nagasaki had sent him. After chatting with Toshiko and Ikuko for an hour or so, he got up to leave. At that point I came down from my study and asked him to stay for dinner. He accepted at once, saying he would be delighted, and settled down comfortably. I went back upstairs while Toshiko prepared the meal. My wife remained in the sitting room with him.

We had nothing special to offer, except his mullet roe and some carp *sushi* that Ikuko bought at the Nishiki market yesterday. Soon we were having these tidbits as an appetizer, with brandy. Ikuko is fond of salty things, particularly carp *sushi*. I don't care for it, nor does Toshiko. Even Kimura, who likes such things, found it a little too strong for him.

Kimura has never brought us a present before today; he seems to have been angling for an invitation to dinner. I wonder what he's after. Which one attracts him, Ikuko or Toshiko? If I were he, and had to say which of the two I found more attractive, I have no doubt that, despite her age, I would choose the mother. But I can't tell about him. Perhaps his real aim is to win Toshiko. Since she seems unenthusiastic, he may be trying to improve his chances by ingratiating himself with Ikuko. . . .

But what am I after, for that matter? Why did I have Kimura stay for dinner again this evening? I must admit that my own attitude has been rather strange. About a week ago, on the seventh, I already had a slight—perhaps not so slight—feeling of jealousy toward him. (Indeed, I think it began several weeks ago, before the end of the year.) Yet isn't it true that I secretly enjoyed it? Such feelings have always given me an erotic stimulus; in a sense, they're both necessary and pleasurable to me. That night, stimulated by jealousy, I succeeded in satisfying Ikuko. I realize that Kimura is becoming indispensable to our sexual life. However, I'd like to warn her, though I need scarcely say it, that she mustn't go too far with him. Not that there shouldn't be an element of danger—the more the better, in fact. I want her to make me insanely jealous. It's all right if she makes me suspicious that she *has* gone too far. I want her to do that.

THE KEY

Even so, she ought to realize that what I ask of her—as difficult, as outrageous as it may seem —is for the sake of her own happiness.

JANUARY 17

•

Kimura hasn't been back, but Ikuko and I drink brandy every evening now. With a little urging, she consumes a surprising amount of it. I like to watch her struggling to stay sober, looking cold and pale; there is something indescribably seductive about her at such times.

Of course my object is to get her drunk and go to bed with her; but why doesn't she yield gracefully? She becomes more and more perverse, won't let me touch her feet. But what she herself wants, she exacts.

JANUARY 20

. .

Today my head ached all day long. It wasn't quite a hangover, though I must have had a little too much last night.

Mr. Kimura seems worried about my drinking. He doesn't like to see me take more than two glasses of brandy. "Don't you think you've had enough?" he asks, trying to discourage me. My husband, on the other hand, keeps offering me more. Apparently he knows my weakness for it, and means to give me all I want. But I've about reached my limit. So far I've managed to go on drinking without letting them see how intoxicated I've become; but I suffer from the aftereffects. I must be more cautious.

JANUARY 28

.

Tonight Ikuko fainted. We were sitting around the dinner table with Kimura, when she suddenly got up and left the room. She didn't return, and

Kimura asked if she might be ill. Knowing that she sometimes goes to hide in the lavatory when she's had too much to drink, I told him I thought she would be back soon. But she was gone so long that he became concerned, and went to look for her.

A moment later he called to Toshiko from the hallway, and asked her to come out. (Again tonight she had hurried through dinner and promptly retired to her room.) "I'm afraid something is wrong," he said. "I can't find your mother anywhere."

But Toshiko found her—found her lying in the deep wooden bathtub, soaking. She was clinging with both hands to the edge of the tub, her head resting on her hands, her eyes closed. Even when Toshiko tried to rouse her, she didn't stir.

Kimura rushed back to tell me. I went to see what was wrong with her. The first thing I did was to take her pulse: it was feeble, beating at only about forty a minute. I undressed, got into the tub myself, picked her up, and carried her out to the adjoining dressing room, where I laid her down on the floor. Toshiko wrapped her in a large bath towel, and said: "I'll see that the bed is ready." Kimura was at a loss to know what to do; he kept fidgeting, darting in and out of the dressing room. When I asked him to help me, he seemed relieved.

"She'll catch cold if we don't dry her off quickly," I said. "Would you mind giving me a hand?" We dried her with fresh towels. (I hadn't forgotten to "use" Kimura. He did the upper half of her body, and I the lower. I was careful to wipe her thoroughly between her toes, and I told Kimura to do the same between her fingers. All the while I kept a sharp watch on him.)

Toshiko brought in a nightgown, but, when she saw Kimura helping, left at once "to get the hot-water bottle." We put Ikuko into the nightgown and carried her to the bedroom.

"It might be cerebral anemia," Kimura said. "Maybe we'd better not give her a hot-water bottle." The three of us discussed whether or not to call a doctor. I was willing to have Dr. Kodama, though I didn't like even him to see my wife in such a disgraceful state. However, because she has a weak heart, I finally asked him to come.

Dr. Kodama confirmed that her trouble was cerebral anemia, but added: "There's no reason

24

to worry." Then he gave her an injection of Vita-camphor. By the time he left, it was two a.m.

JANUARY 29

● ●

I can remember everything that happened last night until the time when I began to feel sick and left the room. I can even dimly recall going for a bath, and fainting in the tub. I'm not sure what happened after that. When I woke up at dawn and looked around I found myself lying in bed. Someone must have carried me here. All day long my head has been so heavy I haven't felt like getting up. I've dozed on and on, waking for a moment and then drifting off into another dream. It's evening, and since I'm feeling a little better, I'm able to write this much. Now I'm going back to sleep.

•

My wife hasn't been up since last night's incident.
It was about midnight when Kimura and I carried
her to the bedroom, half-past twelve when I
called Dr. Kodama, and two o'clock when he left.
I went to the door with him, and saw that it was
a clear, starlit night, but extremely cold. Our bedroom stove usually keeps us comfortable till morning on a single scoopful of coal, which I throw in
before I go to bed; last night, however, at Kimura's
own suggestion, I had him fire it up enough to
make the room quite warm.

"I'll be leaving, then, if there's nothing else
I can do," he said.

I couldn't send him home at that hour.
"Why not stay overnight?" I asked. "I can find
somewhere for you to sleep."

"Please don't bother, sir," he said. "I haven't
far to go." After helping me carry Ikuko in, he
had stood waiting uneasily between our beds (I
was sitting in the only chair). It occurs to me that
Toshiko disappeared just as he came into the bedroom.

He insisted on going home, and left, as I had

hoped he would. A certain plan had been taking shape in my mind for a long time, and I needed privacy to carry it out. Once I was sure he had gone, and that Toshiko wouldn't come in again, I went over and took Ikuko's pulse. It was normal: the Vitacamphor seemed to have worked. As far as I could tell, she was in a deep slumber. Of course she may have been only shamming. But that needn't hinder me, I thought.

I began by firing the stove up even hotter, till it was roaring. Then I slowly drew off the black cloth that I had draped over the shade of the floor lamp. Stealthily I moved the lamp to my wife's bedside, placing it so that she was lying within its circle of light. I felt my heart pound. I was excited to think that what I had so long dreamed of was about to be realized.

Next, I quietly went upstairs to get the fluorescent lamp from my study, brought it back, and put it on the night table. This was by no means a sudden whim. Last fall I replaced my old desk lamp with a fluorescent one, because I foresaw that I might sooner or later have a chance like this. Toshiko and my wife were opposed to it at the time, saying it would affect the radio; but I told them that my eyesight was weakening and

27

THE KEY

the old lamp was hard to read by—which was quite true. However, my real reason was a desire to see Ikuko's naked body in that white radiance. That had been my fantasy ever since I had first heard of fluorescent lighting.

Everything went as I had hoped. I took away her covers, carefully slipped her thin nightgown off, and turned her on her back. She lay there completely naked, exposed to the daylight brilliance of the two lamps. Then I began to study her in detail, as if I were studying a map. For a while, as I gazed on that beautiful, milk-white body, I felt bewildered. It was the first time I had ever had an unimpeded view of her in the nude.

I suppose the average husband is familiar with all the details of his wife's body, down to the very wrinkles on the soles of her feet. But Ikuko has never let me examine her that way. Of course in love-making I have had certain opportunities—but never below the waist, never more than she had to let me see. Only by touch have I been able to picture to myself the beauty of her body, which is why I wanted so desperately to look at her under that brilliant light. And what I saw far exceeded my expectations.

For the first time I was able to enjoy a full

view of her, able to explore all her long-hidden secrets. Ikuko, who was born in 1911, doesn't have the tall, Western kind of figure so common among the young girls of today. Having been an expert swimmer and tennis player, she is well proportioned for a Japanese woman of her age; still, she is not particularly full-bosomed, nor sizable in the buttocks, either. Moreover, her legs, as long and graceful as they are, can hardly be called straight. They bulge out at the calves, and her ankles are not quite trim. But, rather than slim, foreign-looking legs, I have always liked the slightly bowed ones of the old-fashioned Japanese woman, such as my mother and my aunt. Those slender, pipestem legs are uninteresting. And instead of overdeveloped breasts and buttocks, I prefer the gently swelling lines of the Bodhisattva in the Chuguji Temple. I had supposed that my wife's body must be shaped like that, and it turned out that I was right.

What surpassed anything I had imagined was the utter purity of her skin. Most people have at least a minor flaw, some kind of dark spot, a birthmark, mole, or the like; but although I searched her body with the most scrupulous care, I could find no blemish. I turned her face down, and even peered into the hollow where the white flesh of her buttocks swelled up on either side. . . . How extraordinary for a woman to have reached the age of forty-four, and to have experienced childbirth, without suffering the slightest injury to her skin! Never before had I been allowed to gaze at this superb body, but perhaps that is just as well. To be startled, after more than twenty years together, by a first awareness of the physical beauty of one's own wife—that, surely, is to begin a new marriage. We have long since passed the stage of disillusionment, and now I can love her with twice the passion I used to have.

I turned her on her back once again. For a while I stood there, devouring her with my eyes. Suddenly it appeared to me that she was only pretending to be asleep. She had been asleep at first, but had awakened; then, shocked and horrified at what was going on, she had tried to conceal her embarrassment by shamming. . . . Perhaps it was merely my own fantasy, but I wanted to believe it. I was captivated by the idea that this exquisite, fair-skinned body, which I could manipulate as boldly as if it were lifeless, was very much alive, was conscious of everything I did. But suppose that she really *was* asleep—isn't it dangerous for me to write about how I indulged myself with her? I can scarcely doubt that she reads this diary, in which case my revelations may make her decide to stop drinking. . . . No, I don't think so; stopping would confirm that she *does* read it. Otherwise she wouldn't have known what went on while she was unconscious.

For over an hour, beginning at three o'clock, I steeped myself in the pleasure of looking at her. Of course that wasn't all I did. I wanted to find out how far she would let me go, if she were only pretending to be asleep. And I wanted to embarrass her to the point that she would have to continue her pretense to the very end. One by one I tried all the sexual vagaries that she so much loathes—all the tricks that she calls annoying, disgusting, shameful. At last I fulfilled my desire to lavish caresses with my tongue, as freely as I liked, on those beautiful feet. I tried everything I could imagine—things, to use her words, "too shameful to mention."

Once, curious to see how she would respond, I bent over to kiss an especially sensitive place—and happened to drop my glasses on her stomach. Her eyelids fluttered open for a moment, as if she had been startled awake. I was startled too, and hastily switched off the fluorescent lamp. Then I poured some drinking water into a cup, added hot water from the kettle on the stove till it was luke-warm, chewed up a tablet of Luminal and half a tablet of Quadronox in a mouthful of it, and transferred the mixture directly from my mouth to hers. She swallowed it as if in a dream. Some-times a dose of that size doesn't work; but I knew it would give her an excuse for pretending to be asleep.

As soon as I could see that she was sleeping (or at least shamming), I set out to accomplish my final purpose. Since I had already aroused my-self to a state of intense excitement by the most thorough, unhampered preliminaries, I succeeded in performing the act with a vigor that quite astonished me. I was no longer my usual spineless, timid self, but a man powerful enough to subdue her lustfulness. From now on, I thought, I would have to get her drunk as often as possible.

And yet, in spite of the fact that she had had several orgasms, she still seemed to be only half awake. Occasionally she opened her eyes a little, but she would be looking off in another direction. Her hands were moving slowly, languidly, with the dreamlike movements of a somnambulist. Soon, what had never happened before, she began groping as if to explore my chest, arms, cheeks, neck, legs. . . . Up till now she had never touched or looked at any part of me that she could avoid.

It was then that Kimura's name escaped her lips. She said it in a kind of delirious murmur— faintly, very faintly indeed—but she certainly said it. I'm not sure whether she was really delirious or whether that was only a subterfuge. Was she dreaming of making love with Kimura, or was she telling me how much she longed to? Perhaps she was warning me never to humiliate her like this again.

Kimura telephoned around eight this evening to ask about Ikuko. "I should have stopped in to see how she was," he said.

"There's nothing to worry about," I told him. "I've given her a sedative, and she's still asleep."

It's nine o'clock in the morning, and I haven't been out of bed since the night before last. This is Monday; my husband left the house about half an hour ago. Before leaving he tiptoed into the bedroom, but I pretended to be asleep. He listened to my breathing for a moment, kissed my feet again, and went out. Baya came to see how I was feeling. I had her bring me a hot towel. After washing my face briefly, I ordered some milk and a soft-boiled egg. When I asked about Toshiko I was told she was in her room. She didn't make an appearance, though.

I suppose I'm well enough to get up, but I've decided to stay here quietly and write in my diary instead. It's a good chance to think over what has happened. First of all, why on earth did I get so drunk Saturday night? I suppose my physical condition had something to do with it. Then, too, the brandy wasn't our usual Three Stars. My husband had brought home a new kind, a bottle of Courvoisier, "the Brandy of Napoleon." It was so delicious that I soon found I'd had too much. Since I don't like to be seen when I'm intoxicated, I've got into the habit of shutting myself up in the lavatory as soon as I begin to feel unsteady—and I had to again that evening. I must have stayed there twenty or thirty minutes. No, wasn't it closer to an hour, or even two? I didn't feel at all sick. Actually, I felt elated.

My mind was hazy, but it wasn't a complete blank; I remember a few things here and there. I can recall that my back and legs were so tired from squatting over the toilet that before I knew it I was leaning forward on both hands. My head sank down till it touched the floor. Then, feeling saturated with the smell of the lavatory, I got up and left. Maybe I meant to wash off the odor; maybe I simply didn't want to join the others while I was still unsteady. In any case, I seem to have gone directly to the bath and taken off my clothes. I say "seem" because it lingers in my mind like the events of an old dream; but I have no idea what happened after that. (I wonder if they called Dr. Kodama. There's adhesive tape on my upper right arm, so I must have had an injection.)

When I came to, I was in my bed, and early-morning sunlight was filtering into the room. It must have been around six o'clock, but I can't say

I was fully conscious from then on. All day yesterday I had a splitting headache and felt my whole body sinking heavily, deeply down. Time after time I woke up and then dropped off to sleep again—no, I was never really awake or asleep; all day long I drifted between the two. My head was throbbing, but I kept finding myself in a strange world that made me forget the pain.

Surely *that* was a dream; but could a dream have been quite so vivid, so lifelike? At first I was amazed to feel myself reaching the climax of an excruciatingly keen pleasure, a kind of sensual fulfillment beyond anything I could expect from my husband. Soon, though, I knew that the man with whom I was in bed was not my husband. It was Kimura-san. Had he stayed overnight to help take care of me? Where had my husband gone? Was it all right for me to behave so immorally?

But the pleasure was too intense to let me dwell on such things. Never in more than twenty years of marriage had my husband given me an experience like that. How dull and monotonous it had always been—dreary, stale, leaving a disagreeable aftertaste. I realized that never before— not until that moment—had I known true sexual intercourse. Kimura-san had taught me. . . . . Yet I realized, too, that I was partly dreaming. Somehow I was aware that the man embracing me only seemed to be Kimura-san, that he was actually my husband.

I suppose he carried me here from the bath that night, put me to bed, and then, since I was still unconscious, amused himself with me in all sorts of ways. Once, when he was kissing me roughly under my arms, I was startled awake. He had dropped his glasses on me; my eyes opened the instant I felt their chilly touch. All my clothes had been stripped off, and I was lying on my back, stark naked, exposed to a hideous glare of light. There were two lamps: the floor lamp and another—a fluorescent one—on the bedside table. (Possibly the brightness awakened me.) I lay there vacantly. He picked up his glasses and put them on; then, leaving my arms, he began kissing me further down, below my waist. I remember shrinking away instinctively as I groped for a blanket. He noticed I'd begun to stir, and pulled some covers over me. Then he turned off the fluorescent lamp and draped something over the other one.

We don't keep a fluorescent lamp in the bedroom: he had to bring it from his study. I feel myself blush to think how he must have enjoyed exploring my body under that glaring light. He must have seen places that even I have never looked at so closely. I'm sure I was left naked for hours; he'd fired the stove up till the room was suffocatingly warm so that I wouldn't catch cold —and wouldn't awaken. It makes me angry and ashamed to think what he did with me, though at the time what bothered me most was the throbbing ache in my head. He chewed up some tablets (probably sleeping pills) in a sip of water, and gave them to me mouth to mouth. I swallowed obediently, to get rid of the pain. Soon I began losing consciousness again, drifting off into a half-sleep.

And then I had the illusion of holding Kimura-san in my arms. But is "illusion" the right word for it? Doesn't that suggest something nebulous floating in the air, ready to fade out of sight at any moment? What I saw and felt was not so intangible, not just an illusion of holding him in my arms. Even now that sensation lingers in the flesh of my arms and thighs. It's entirely unlike the feel of my husband's embrace. With these arms I grasped Kimura-san's strong young arms as

38

he pressed me tight against his firm, resilient body. I remember that his skin seemed dazzlingly fair, not the usual dark skin of a Japanese.

And I thought—I'm ashamed to confess it, though I'm sure my husband doesn't even know about this diary, much less read it—if only *he* could make me feel this way! Why can't he be like this? . . . Yet, oddly enough, I somehow knew all along that I was dreaming, or mingling dream and reality. I knew I was in my husband's arms, and that he only reminded me of Kimura-san. But the amazing thing is that I kept on having that feeling of pressure, of completion, a feeling I can't associate with him.

If it's the Courvoisier that brought me that illusion, I'd like to have it often. I'm grateful to my husband for the experience. Still, I wonder how much truth there was in my dream of Kimura-san. Why should he have appeared to me that way, since I've never seen him except when he's fully dressed? Is the real Kimura-san different from the one I've imagined? Sometime—not just in my imagination—I'd like to find out what he's *really* like.

•

Kimura telephoned me at school today, shortly past noon, and asked how my wife was getting along. I told him that she was still asleep when I left the house, but that she seemed to be all right. And I suggested he come over for a drink this evening.

"For a drink!" he exclaimed. "Not after what happened the other night. If you'll excuse me for saying so, I think you and your wife ought to be a little more abstemious, sir. But I'll stop in to see how she is."

He arrived at four o'clock. Ikuko was up by then, and came to the sitting room. He said that he couldn't stay, but I insisted. "Let's have a drink to make up for last time," I told him. "You needn't be in such a hurry."

Ikuko was smiling too. Certainly she didn't show any disapproval. In fact, Kimura himself seemed to want to stay. I'm sure he didn't realize what had gone on in our bedroom after he left that night (I had even returned the fluorescent lamp to my study by the next morning); nor could he possibly have known that he had invaded my wife's fantasies, and had enraptured her. Yet why did he give the impression of being eager to have her drink again? He seemed to know what she wanted. If he *did* know, was it by intuition, or had she actually given him a hint? Only Toshiko looked displeased when the three of us began drinking. She finished her dinner quickly and went out.

Again tonight Ikuko left the room, hid in the lavatory, and then went to take a bath and collapsed in the tub. We usually heat the bath every other day, but she has told Baya that we would like it daily, for the present. Since Baya lives out, she fills the tub before going home, and one of us lights the gas under it. Tonight Ikuko lit it, just in time.

Everything happened exactly as it did the other night. Dr. Kodama came and gave her an injection of camphor; Toshiko slipped off somewhere; Kimura helped me with her, and then left. My own later actions were the same, too. Strangest of all, she murmured Kimura's name again— was she having that same dream, that same delusion, just as she had had before? Should I, perhaps, interpret it as a kind of ridicule?

41

• •

Today Toshiko asked if she could live away from home. She said she's been wanting a quiet place to study, and that a convenient one has just turned up. It was suggested to her by Madame Okada, an old Frenchwoman who used to be her teacher at Doshisha and who still gives her private lessons. Madame Okada's Japanese husband is bedridden with paralysis; she supports him by teaching French. Since his illness, though, she hasn't done much tutoring: Toshiko is the only student who comes to her home. The house isn't a large one, but they have no children, and they don't need the garden cottage that used to be her husband's study. If Toshiko cares to take it, Madame Okada will feel safer whenever she has to be away.

Nothing would please them more, it seems, than to have Toshiko as a tenant. They'll give her a telephone; she's to bring her piano if she likes (the floor beams can be strengthened by laying bricks); a passageway can even be added, quite easily, so that she'll have direct access to the lavatory and the bath, without having to go through the rest of the house. People seldom

42

telephone them while Madame Okada is out. In any case, Toshiko is to pay no attention to such things; they'll see that she isn't bothered.

Besides all this, the rent will be very cheap. Toshiko has said she'd like to try it for a while.

Maybe she's disgusted because Kimura-san has been coming over to drink with us every three or four days (we've already emptied another bottle of Courvoisier), and because I've fainted in the bathtub every time. I'm sure she's noticed— and been curious about it—that her parents' room often blazes with light in the early-morning hours. But I can't tell if that's really why she wants to move or if she has some other reason, which she's hiding.

"Go ask Papa yourself, and see what he says," I told her. "If Papa says it's all right, I won't object."

FEBRUARY 14

•

Today Kimura said something unexpected to me while Ikuko was in the kitchen. He asked if I had

43

ever heard of a "Polaroid camera." It seems to be an American invention—a camera that develops and prints its own photographs. They use it to make the still pictures they show on television at the end of *sumo* wrestling bouts, to help explain the fine points of the winning hold. According to him, the camera is very easy to operate—as easy as an ordinary one—and easy to carry, too. If you use a Strob flash, you can take pictures without a tripod.

Polaroid cameras are still quite rare in Japan, Kimura told me; even the film itself (printing-paper superimposed on negative) has to be specially imported. However, a friend of his happens to have one, with plenty of film. "If you'd care to use it, I can borrow it for you," he said.

As he spoke, an idea came to me. But how did he guess that I would be pleased to learn about such a camera? That puzzles me. He does seem remarkably well acquainted with what goes on at our house.

• •

A disturbing thing happened a little while ago, about four o'clock this afternoon. I hide my diary in a drawer of the cabinet here in the sitting room (a drawer no one else uses), stuffed in under layers of old papers—personal documents, letters from my parents, and so on. I don't like to take it out while my husband is at home, but occasionally I want to jot something down before I forget it, or I simply have an urge to write. And so I steal a few minutes when he's shut up in his study, without waiting for him to leave the house. The study is over this room; I can't hear him, but somehow I feel aware of what he's doing—of whether he's reading, writing in his own diary, or perhaps just sitting there lost in thought. I suppose he feels the same way about me. The study is always deathly quiet, but now and then—or so I imagine—a peculiar hush falls; he seems to be holding his breath and concentrating on the room below. Such moments are apt to occur when I'm writing. I don't think that is only my imagination.

In order not to make any noise I use a

writing-brush instead of a pen, and I've folded sheets of delicate rice paper into a small Japanese-style notebook. But this afternoon I became so absorbed in my diary that I momentarily relaxed my guard—something I've never done before. Just then, on purpose or not, my husband came silently down the stairs. He passed the sitting room without stopping in, went to the lavatory, and returned immediately to his study. I say "silently" because that was my impression. Maybe he didn't try to soften his footsteps; maybe I'd have noticed them if I hadn't been so preoccupied. Anyway, I didn't hear him until he reached the bottom of the stairs. I was leaning over the table, writing, but I hastily put the diary and brush case out of sight. (I don't use an ink-stone. The brush case—an antique Chinese one my father gave me—holds ink too.) So I escaped being caught in the act.

But, in thrusting the notebook under a cushion, I crumpled a few of its thin leaves. I wonder if he heard that slight rustle, so characteristic of rice paper. I'm sure he did. If he heard it he must have recognized the sound, in which case he may have guessed what I'm using that sort of paper for. I shall have to be more careful. Supposing

46

he's already guessed I keep a diary: what can I do about it? Even if I change the hiding place, there's nowhere really safe in this little room. I'll just have to try not to leave the house while he's here. For days now my head has been feeling so heavy that I haven't gone out as often as usual; I've left most of the shopping to Toshiko or Baya. But Kimura-san has asked if I'd like to go see *Le Rouge et le Noir* at the Asahi Theater. I *would* like to. In the meantime I'll have to think of a plan.

FEBRUARY 18

•

Last night makes the fourth time that I have heard my wife call out Kimura's name. By now it's obvious that she is shamming. Why should she do such a thing? Perhaps she means to inform me that she is not really asleep—but how should I interpret *that*? Is it: "I want to think my partner is Kimura-san so that I can become really passionate. After all, it's to your benefit"? Or is it: "I'm simply trying to stimulate you by arousing

47

your jealousy. No matter what happens, I am an unwaveringly faithful wife"?

Today Toshiko finally moved to the cottage at Madame Okada's house. The telephone isn't in yet, but the work of reinforcing the floor and building a passageway has been nearly finished. Because this was supposed to be an unlucky day, Ikuko had asked her to wait till the twenty-first, a propitious one. Toshiko refused.

The piano will be moved early next week. With Kimura's help, Toshiko has already taken most of her other things. (By the time Ikuko got up—after last night's party—there was hardly anything left to do.) It seems that Madame Okada lives in the Sekidencho district, a few blocks west of Kyoto University, about five minutes' walk from here. Since Kimura has a room near Hyakumamben, he is a good deal nearer Sekidencho than we are.

As soon as he arrived today he called from the stairs to ask if he could see me for a moment, and then came up to my study. "I've brought what I promised," he said, handing me the Polaroid camera.

• •

I cannot imagine what is in Toshiko's mind. She seems to love her mother, and yet hate her. But there's no doubt that she hates her father. Apparently she misunderstands our marital relations, and thinks it's he, not I, who has a lustful nature. She seems to think he forces me to satisfy his sexual demands, though I'm really too weak for it, and that he's addicted to coarse, perverted pleasures, which I'm dragged into against my will. (I must admit I've tried to give her that impression.) Yesterday when she came to pick up the last of her things she stopped in my bedroom to warn me.

"You're going to let Papa kill you!" she said abruptly, and left.

That was extraordinary for a girl like her, who's as reticent as I am. She *does* seem to worry that my chest trouble may be aggravated, and to hate her father on that account. Yet the way she uttered that warning made it sound oddly scornful, full of spite and malice. I can't believe she was saying it out of the warm feeling of a daughter anxious about her mother. Isn't she in-

49

wardly resentful of the fact that although she's twenty years younger she's not as attractive as I am in face or figure? From the very first she said she disliked Mr. Kimura; maybe that was because he reminded her of an actor I'm fond of. She may have deliberately hidden her real feelings, and pretended to dislike him. I wonder if she isn't secretly hostile to me.

Although I try not to leave the house, sooner or later I may have to—and my husband may come home one day when he's supposed to be teaching. I've been racking my brains about what to do with this diary. If it's useless to hide it, at least I'd like to know if he's reading it on the sly. And so I've decided to use a telltale mark of some kind. Maybe it would be all the better if it's one that only I know about, one he won't recognize; but maybe he'll stop spying if he realizes that his wife knows what he's up to. (I'm afraid that's very doubtful, though.) Even so, it's not easy to hit on the right kind of mark. I may succeed once, but I can scarcely repeat it safely. For instance, I can stick a toothpick between the pages somewhere so that it will fall out when the book is opened. The first time may go smoothly enough, but after that he'll note which pages it lies between, and put it back the same way. He's quite clever about such things. Yet I can't invent a new method every time.

After a good deal of thought, I decided to cut a length of No. 600 Scotch tape, measure it, and use it to seal together the two covers of the notebook. (I'll measure its distance from the top and bottom of the book too. Next time I'll make a slight change in its length and in the place where I apply it.) He'll have to peel it off to look inside. Of course it's not impossible for him to cut a new tape of the same size and replace the old one, exactly as it was. But that would be an awfully delicate task; I really don't see how he could do it. Besides, when he removes the tape, no matter how carefully, he's sure to mar the cover a little. Luckily, it's thick, white-glazed Hosho paper, which is easily damaged. A few millimeters of the surface will come off with the tape here and there. I don't think he'll be able to read my diary without leaving some trace.

•

Kimura has had no ostensible reason to visit us since Toshiko moved out, but he still comes over quite regularly, every three or four days. I often telephone him myself. Toshiko stops in almost daily, but doesn't stay.

I have already used the Polaroid camera twice. I've taken full front and back views of Ikuko's body, as well as detailed shots of every part of it, from the most alluring angles: I have pictures of her bending, stretching, twisting, pictures of her with her arms and legs contorted into all manner of poses.

As to why I take such photographs: first of all, I enjoy taking them. I derive great pleasure from creating these poses, freely manipulating her while she sleeps (or pretends to). My second reason is to paste them in my diary so that she will see them. Then, certainly, she will discover— and be amazed at—the unsuspected beauty of her own body. A third reason is to show her why I am so desperately eager to look at her in the nude. I want her to understand me—perhaps even be sympathetic. (I dare say it is unheard of for a man of fifty-five to be so fascinated by his forty-four-year-old wife. She would do well to think of that.) Finally, I want to humiliate her in the extreme, to see how long she will go on playing innocent.

Unfortunately, this camera has a rather slow lens, and no range finder; since I'm not very good at estimating distances, my pictures are often out of focus. I understand that there is a new, highly sensitive Polaroid film, but it's hard to get. The kind Kimura brought is old, past its expiration date. You can't expect good results from it. Furthermore, it's bothersome to have to use a flash.

Since I can hardly fulfill my second and third purposes with this camera, I won't paste the photographs in, for the time being.

FEBRUARY 27

• •

It's Sunday. Kimura-san came over at nine thirty this morning and asked if I wouldn't like to see *Le Rouge et le Noir* today. Sundays are best for him just now, he says; during the week he's busy helping students get ready for their college entrance examinations. In March things will be more leisurely, but this month he often has to stay late at school and give extra lessons. Even after he goes home he's sometimes visited by outside students who want him to tutor them. He's said to be sharp-witted, an expert at spotting questions. I think I can understand why they say that. I don't know how much of a scholar he is, but for sheer perception my husband is no match for him.

Since my husband stays home on Sunday, it's not convenient for me to go out. But Kimura-san had spoken to Toshiko on his way over. Soon she arrived, and asked me to join them. She looked as if she was thinking: "I don't want to go, but it might be awkward for the two of you, so I'll sacrifice myself for your sake and come along."

"You have to be early on Sunday," said Kimura-san, "or you won't get a seat, you know."

My husband urged me, too. "I'll be home all day," he said. "Go on: I'll look after the house. You said you wanted to see it, didn't you?"

I knew why he was encouraging me, but I was prepared for the situation, and I agreed to go.

We got to the theater at half-past ten, and came out a little after one. I asked Toshiko and Kimura-san to stop in for lunch, but they refused. Although my husband had said he'd be home all day, he went out for a walk about three o'clock and stayed away the rest of the afternoon. As soon as he was gone I took out my diary and examined it. The Scotch tape didn't seem any different, nor, at first glance, did the cover. But when I looked through a magnifying glass I found two or three faint blemishes—the tape had been peeled off expertly—which couldn't be hidden. I'd made doubly sure by leaving a toothpick inside, counting the leaves to know where I'd inserted it. Now it was in a different place.

There is no longer the slightest doubt that my husband has read this diary. Should I give it up, then? I began it solely for the purpose of talking to myself, since I don't like to open my heart to another person. Now that it's obviously being read by someone else, I suppose I ought to abandon it. Yet the "someone" is my own husband, and we have an unspoken agreement to behave as if we weren't aware of each other's secrets. So perhaps I shall go on with it after all. I'll use it to talk to him indirectly, to say things I

55

THE KEY

couldn't possibly tell him to his face. But even if he *is* reading it, I do hope he'll keep that to himself. Of course he's not the sort to admit it, anyway.

No matter what he does, I want him to know that I am definitely not reading *his* diary. He ought to realize that I'm very old-fashioned, a woman who's been carefully brought up, who wouldn't dream of infringing on anyone's privacy. I know where my husband's diary is; sometimes I have touched it; once in a great while I may even have opened it and looked inside. But I have never read a word of it. That is the simple truth.

FEBRUARY 27

•

I was right after all! Ikuko has been keeping a diary. I haven't mentioned this before, but the fact is, I got an inkling of it several days ago. The other afternoon as I was on my way to the lavatory I glanced into the sitting room, and saw her leaning awkwardly over the table. A moment before, I had heard a rustling sound, as if rice paper were

56

being crumpled. Not just a sheet or two—it sounded as if a substantial packet of it, a bound volume, perhaps, had been hastily shoved out of sight under a cushion. We seldom use rice paper at our house: it wasn't hard to imagine what she would be doing with that soft, discreet paper.

However, I had no chance to investigate until today. While she was at the movies I searched the sitting room, and easily found it. What astonished me, though, was that she had evidently expected me to go looking for it, and had sealed it with Scotch tape. A ridiculous thing for her to do! The degree of that woman's suspiciousness is really shocking. She ought to know that even though it's my own wife's diary I'm not such a sneak as to read it without permission. Yet I couldn't help feeling annoyed, and wondering if it might be possible to peel the tape off so skillfully that she would never detect it. I wanted to say: "Your tape is useless! That won't keep your diary safe—you'll have to think of a better way!"

But I failed. As I might have imagined, she was too much for me. Although I tried to peel the tape off with the most scrupulous care, it left a slight blemish on the cover. I realized then how foolish I had been. No doubt she had even measured the tape, but I had thoughtlessly rolled it into a ball. I sealed the diary up again with a piece that seemed to be about the same length. It's not likely to deceive her.

Still, I can assure her that although I unsealed her diary—even opened it and looked inside—I didn't read a single word of it. It's hard for a near-sighted person like myself to read such a tiny script, anyway. I hope she will believe me. Of course, with her, the more I deny it, the more she will think I'm guilty. Perhaps, if I am to be blamed in any case, I might just as well have read it. But I didn't. In fact, I am afraid to know what she may have said about her true feelings toward Kimura. Ikuko, I beg of you, don't confess! Even though I'll not see it, don't make such a confession! Lie, if you must, but say that you're only using him for my sake, that he means nothing more to you.

Kimura came to take Ikuko to the movies this morning, because I had asked him to. Some time ago I told him I'd noticed that she scarcely leaves the house. "Lately she has Baya do all the errands," I said. "It's not like her—I wish you'd take her out somewhere for a few hours."

As usual, Toshiko went along. I don't suppose that she had any special reason for joining them, though it's difficult to interpret her actions. Toshiko is even more complicated than her mother, in some respects. I wonder if she is resentful because, unlike most fathers, I seem to be less devoted to her than I am to her mother. If that is what she thinks, she's wrong; I love them equally. Only, I love them in different ways—no father could feel quite *that* way about his daughter. I'll have to see that she understands this.

Tonight, for the first time since Toshiko moved out, the four of us sat around the dinner table together. Toshiko left early; Ikuko had her usual reaction to brandy. Later, when Kimura was leaving, I gave the Polaroid camera back to him.

"It's quite an advantage not having to worry about developing the negatives," I said. "But I don't like using a flash—maybe I'd be better off with an ordinary camera. I think I'll try our Zeiss Ikon."

"Will you send the film out?" he asked.

I had already given that a good deal of thought. "Do you suppose you could develop it for me?" I said.

He looked a little embarrassed, and asked if I couldn't do it here. I told him that I believed he knew what kind of photographs I was taking. He said he wasn't sure.

"They're not the sort I'd care to let anyone else see," I went on, "but I can't very well develop them at home. I want some enlargements, too—and we don't have a good place for a darkroom. Couldn't you make one at your house? I'd rather not let a stranger handle them."

"We may have a place for one, somewhere," he answered. "I'll speak to my landlord about it."

FEBRUARY 28

•

Kimura came over at eight this morning, while Ikuko was still fast asleep. He said he was stopping in on his way to school. I had been in bed too, but when I heard his voice I got up and came to the sitting room.

"It's all right!" he announced. I wondered what was all right; it turned out to be the darkroom. Since their laundry room is not in use just now, he can have it whenever he wants. It will

60

make an excellent darkroom, with running water.

I told him to get it ready immediately.

MARCH 3

•

Kimura says he is busy with examinations, but he is more conscientious than I am. . . . Last night I took out the Zeiss Ikon for the first time in years, and shot an entire roll of film—thirty-six exposures. He stopped in again today, as nonchalant as ever. "May I see you a moment?" he asked, then came into my study and looked at me inquiringly.

As a matter of fact, I still hadn't made up my mind to entrust the developing to him. He was clearly the one person for the job, since by now seeing Ikuko in the nude was scarcely a novelty for him. Yet even he had only caught fleeting glimpses of her naked body; he had never seen it in all those varied, seductive poses. Wouldn't the photographs be likely to excite him? That was no concern of mine, to be sure; but mightn't it lead

61

to something more? If it did, I would have only myself to blame.

Besides, I had to consider the possibility that he might show her the photographs. She would certainly be indignant (or pretend to be), not only because I had taken them, and without her knowledge, but because I had had someone else develop them. She might even reason that, having already been exposed to Kimura in such a shameful state by her own husband, she had tacit permission to commit adultery with him.

I had let my imagination go so far that I was beginning to feel agonizingly jealous, a feeling so intense, so voluptuous, that it made me eager to accept the risk. I gave Kimura the film, and told him I wanted him to do it all himself. "Be sure no one else sees them," I said. "When you finish, I'll pick out the ones I'd like to have you enlarge."

He must have been brimming over with excitement, but he didn't betray it. "I'll take care of everything," he agreed, and left at once.

• •

Today—for the second time this year—the key was lying by the bookshelf in my husband's study. The first time was on the fourth of January; I'd gone in to clean, and found it in front of the vase of daffodils. This morning, noticing that the Chinese plum blossoms had withered, I went in to replace them with white camellias, and saw the key lying in the very same place. Something is up, I thought; but when I opened the drawer and took out his diary I was startled to find it sealed with tape, just as I had sealed mine. That was his way of saying: "Be sure to open it!"

My husband keeps his diary in an ordinary student's notebook with a smooth, hard cover, not so easily marred as mine. Curious to see if I could peel off the tape—merely out of curiosity—I tried it. As careful as I was, I left some faint scratches after all. Even on that hard surface I couldn't help it. It wouldn't have mattered along the edge of the tape, but little flaws spread all around; there was no way to conceal them. I stuck a new tape on; of course he'll notice that, and be convinced I've read what is inside. But, as I've said over and over again, I swear I've never read a word of it. I suppose what he really wants is to tell me those indecent things that he knows I don't like to hear. And that's why I'm all the more loath to read it.

I hurriedly opened his diary and looked to see how much he had written. Of course that was out of curiosity too. I leafed through the pages filled with his delicate, nervous scrawl—as if the lines were so many ant tracks. But today I found that he had pasted in some obscene photographs. I shut my eyes, and quickly turned the page. Where on earth had he got such pictures, and why had he put them in? Did he want me to see them? I wondered who the woman could be.

Just then an extremely repugnant thought occurred to me. Lately, in the middle of the night, I've dreamed of an occasional blinding flash lighting up the whole room for an instant, as if by a flash bulb. Someone—my husband or Kimura-san —seemed to be photographing me. Maybe it wasn't a dream. Maybe my husband—surely it couldn't have been Kimura-san—was actually taking pictures. I remember that he once said: "You don't know how superb your own body is. I'd like to photograph it and show you." Yes, I'm sure those were pictures of *me*.

Often when I'm in that dazed sleep I have the feeling that I've been stripped naked. Until now I've thought it might be another of my fantasies, but if those are photographs of me it must really happen. Yet I don't even object to his picture-taking, so long as I'm not aware of it. I couldn't possibly allow such a thing while I'm awake; still, since he finds such pleasure in seeing me in the nude, I suppose that as a dutiful wife I ought to let him enjoy himself. In the old days a virtuous woman simply obeyed her husband's wishes, no matter how indecent or how disgusting. She did as she was told, there was no question about it. And I have all the more reason to indulge him if it's true he can't satisfy me unless he's stimulated by crazy pranks like that. It's not just a matter of fulfilling my duty. In return for being a virtuous, submissive wife, I'm able to gratify my own strong sexual appetite.

Even so, why isn't he content with looking at me? I don't see why he should want to take photographs of me in that state and then paste them in his notebook, where I can find them. He ought to know perfectly well that I'm the kind of person in whose heart lustfulness and shyness exist side by side. And I wonder who developed them for him.

THE KEY

Did he have to let another man look at them? Was that just a nasty trick on me, or does it mean something? He's always jeering at my "refinement"—is he trying, now, to break me of that tiresome attitude?

MARCH 10

•

I don't know whether I ought to mention this in my diary, or what it may lead to if Ikuko reads it. But I must confess to a feeling that I have been bringing on a serious mental or physical disorder of some kind. I call it "a feeling" because I suppose that my trouble may be nothing more than a minor neurosis.

Looking back, I think it is fair to say that I haven't always been deficient in sexual vigor. Since middle age, however, my vitality has been sapped by my wife's inordinate demands on it; my desire has become feeble. No, the desire is there, but the strength to back it up has waned. And so I struggle to cope with my oversexed wife,

66

whetting my appetite by all sorts of violent, un-natural methods. Sometimes it frightens me, and I wonder how long this can go on. For about ten years I was a spineless husband, overwhelmed by my wife's energy, but now all that has changed. Now, thanks to the discovery that brandy and Kimura are sovereign remedies, I am impelled by a lust so powerful that it seems almost miracu-lous, even to me. Moreover, I replenish my vital-ity by taking male hormones once a month, as prescribed by Dr. Noma at my request. And to make sure of being sufficiently potent—I do this without his knowledge, administering it myself—I also have injections of five hundred units of an-terior pituitary hormones every four or five days.

Still, I suspect that my extraordinary new vigor is not so much due to drugs as to mental stimulation. The fermenting passion that comes from jealousy, the sexual impulses quickened by feasting my eyes on her nakedness—these things are driving me beyond all self-control, driving me to madness. Now I am the insatiable one. Night after night I immerse myself in undreamed-of ecstasies. I cannot help being grateful for my happiness; at the same time, I have a premonition

67

that it will end, that someday I must pay for it, that moment by moment I am whittling away my life.

Indeed, I have already more than once had certain symptoms, mental as well as physical, which seem to foreshadow that retribution. Last Monday morning—the morning Kimura stopped in on his way to school—a strange thing happened. I had just got out of bed, and was about to go to the sitting room, when I noticed a faint doubling of the outlines of the stove chimney, the sliding doors and screens, the transom, the pillars —of everything around me. I rubbed my eyes, wondering if they were blurred with age. But that wasn't it. Evidently some abnormal change in my vision had taken place. In recent summers I have had mild attacks of dizziness from cerebral anemia, but this was obviously not the same. Unlike those attacks, which only lasted a few minutes, my double vision has been persistent. All lines— even the ribs of the sliding screens and the interstices of the tiles in the bath—seem doubled, and slightly bent. The doubling and the distortion are very slight, not enough to hamper movement or make me attract attention by any clumsiness; and

68

so I have tried to disregard them. But even now the condition remains.

It is true that I haven't suffered any inconvenience or pain; yet I can't deny feeling uneasy. I have thought of going to be examined at the eye clinic, but that rather frightens me; I feel that it's not just something wrong with my eyes —the real disease lies in a more vital place. Besides, although this is probably caused by nervousness, I sometimes totter and almost lose my balance. I seem to be on the verge of falling. I don't know where the nerves that control the sense of equilibrium run, but it always feels as if there is a cavity in the back of my head, directly above the spine, a kind of pivot from which my body swings to one side or the other.

Yesterday I noticed another symptom, though I suppose that it too may be only a neurotic one. Around three in the afternoon, when I wanted to call up Kimura, I couldn't remember the telephone number of his school, a number I call nearly every day. Of course I have had lapses of memory before, but this wasn't ordinary forgetfulness: it was closer to amnesia. I couldn't even remember the exchange. I was startled and disconcerted. Tentatively, I tried to think of the name of the school, but that was no use either. What surprised me most was that I had forgotten Kimura's first name. Even our housekeeper's name was beyond me. To be sure, I hadn't forgotten "Ikuko" and "Toshiko," but the names of Ikuko's father and mother eluded me. As for the woman from whom Toshiko is renting a cottage, I remembered that she was French, that she had a Japanese husband, and that she taught at Doshisha University—but her name wouldn't come to me. Worse yet, I couldn't recall the name of our own street. All I knew was that we lived in the Sakyo ward of Kyoto.

A terrible anxiety gripped me. If this went on, gradually becoming more severe, I would soon be disqualified from my professorship. Not only that, I might become an invalid, house-bound, cut off from society. For the time being, however, my loss of memory has affected chiefly the names of people and places; I haven't forgotten the circumstances concerning them. I couldn't think of the Frenchwoman's name, but I realized that there was such a person, and that Toshiko was renting a cottage from her. In short, only the nerves that transmit names were paralyzed; it wasn't a paralysis of the entire system controlling perception and communication. Fortunately, too, the paralysis lasted only about half an hour. Before long the blocked nerve channels were reopened, my lost memory returned, and, except for my vision, I was back to normal.

In spite of my anxiety at not knowing how long·it might last, I had managed to survive it without telling anyone, without even letting it be noticed. And now, although I have had no trouble since, I am still haunted by the fear that at any moment I may have another attack—the fear that this one may last, not for half an hour, but for a day, a year, perhaps for the rest of my life.

But what if Ikuko reads this, what will she be likely to do? Will she worry about me, and try to control her sexual instinct? I hardly think so. Even if her reason demanded it, her insatiable body would refuse to comply. Short of my collapse, she will never stop insisting on gratification.

Doubtless she will ask herself why I am writing this. "He seemed to be doing so well lately," she will think; "but he's been forced to give in, hasn't he? I suppose he means to frighten me, so that I'll be less demanding."

No, I too have lost all self-restraint. By nature I am a coward about illness, not the sort of person to take risks. Yet now, at fifty-five, I feel that I have at last found something to live for. In some respects I have become even bolder than she.

MARCH 14

• •

Toshiko came over this morning while my husband was out. "I have something to discuss with you," she declared, looking serious. When I asked her what it was, she stared right into my eyes and said: "Yesterday I saw those pictures at Mr. Kimura's."

I didn't understand, and asked her to explain. "Mama, I'm on your side, no matter what," she said. "I wish you'd tell me the truth."

It seems Kimura-san promised to lend her a certain French book; yesterday, happening to pass his house, she stopped to get it. He wasn't there, but she went in anyway, and took the book from the shelf. When she opened it she found a number of photographs.

72

"Mama, what does it all mean?" she asked. I told her I didn't know what she was talking about, and she accused me of trying to deceive her. I gathered that the photographs were the same as those disgraceful ones I saw in my husband's diary the other day—and, just as I guessed, that they were photographs of me. But I couldn't think of a quick explanation. I suppose Toshiko imagined that a real scandal, something far worse than what had actually happened, was at the bottom of it. No doubt those pictures looked like evidence of illicit relations between Kimura-san and myself. For his sake, as well as for my husband's and my own, I should have tried to clear it up at once. But even if I'd been completely frank with her I don't think she'd have believed me.

I hesitated a moment, and said: "It may be hard to believe, but until you told me just now, I didn't really know there *were* any such photographs of me. If there are, Papa took them while I was in a stupor, and all Mr. Kimura did was develop them for him. There's absolutely nothing else between us. I leave it to your imagination why Papa should get me into a state like that, why he should take such pictures and have Mr. Kimura develop them instead of doing it himself. I've already told you as much as I can bear to, even if you are my own daughter. Please don't ask anything more. And please believe that I was only obeying your father. I do whatever he wants, even against my will, because I consider it my duty. It may be hard for you to understand, but to a person like myself, brought up on the old morality, there's no choice in the matter. If he's so eager to have nude photographs of me, I'm willing to swallow my shame and expose myself to the camera—especially if he's the one who operates it."

Toshiko was shocked. "Do you really mean that?" she asked. I said of course I did. "Mama, you're contemptible!" she burst out. I began to suspect I'd enjoyed offending her, and had somewhat exaggerated my true feelings.

"You think you're a model wife," she went on, with a cold, derisive smile. "Is that it?" Apparently she couldn't understand her father's motives, either. Having another man develop the films seemed utterly incomprehensible to her. She said he had humiliated me and tormented Mr. Kimura without any reason, and she kept on denouncing him till I interrupted her.

"I won't have you meddling in this!" I told her. "You say Papa humiliated me, but are you

74

really so sure he did? I don't feel that way about it. Even now he's passionately in love with me—I suppose he had to convince himself that I look young and beautiful for my age. That may seem abnormal, but I can understand it." Because I felt a need to defend him I was able to say things I ordinarily couldn't have. And I did it rather skillfully, I think. Maybe it's just as well for him to read this, and have some appreciation of how I've tried to shield him.

"I wonder if that was all," said Toshiko. "Papa was certainly being sadistic, knowing how Mr. Kimura feels about you."

I didn't answer that. She said she couldn't believe those photographs had been left in the book out of sheer carelessness—"since it was Mr. Kimura who did it." She thought it meant something: maybe he wanted her to perform some function. And she told me some other things she'd observed about him, things it might be better not to repeat here.

•

It was after ten o'clock when I got home tonight, because of the party for Sasaki. It seems that Ikuko had been out all evening. I thought she was at the movies, and went upstairs to work. At eleven she still hadn't returned.

Finally, at eleven thirty, Toshiko phoned. She told me she was calling from Sekidencho, and asked me to come over for a moment.

"Where is Mama?" I asked.

"She's here," Toshiko said.

"It's getting late," I said. "Tell your mother to come home. Baya's already left."

She lowered her voice. "Mama's fainted in the bath. Shall we call Dr. Kodama?" I asked who was there, and she said: "The three of us." Then she added: "I'll explain later. Anyway, I think Mama needs an injection. If you can't come, I'll get Dr. Kodama."

"Don't bother calling him," I said. "I'll be over to take care of it.

These days I make sure to keep the Vita-camphor solution on hand. I took some and left at once. Suddenly a wave of fear passed over me. Suppose my memory failed again!

I knew where to find the house, but this was the first time I had ever visited it. When I arrived, Toshiko was waiting for me inside the gate. She led me through the garden to the cottage, then excused herself and left.

Kimura greeted me apologetically. I didn't ask him for an explanation—nor did he volunteer one. It was an awkward moment for both of us, and I hurriedly set about preparing to give the injection. Bedding had been spread out on the floor-mats in front of the piano, and Ikuko lay there asleep. The tea table beside her was littered with plates and glasses. Her kimono and sash were hanging on the wall nearby, dangling from the ribbon-bedecked hangers that Toshiko uses for Western-style clothes; she was sleeping in her thin silk underrobe. Ikuko has rather showy tastes for her age, but that underrobe seemed especially gaudy. Perhaps I was struck by it because of the unusual time and place.

Her pulse was about as I had expected under the circumstances. All Kimura said was: "Your daughter and I carried her here together." Evidently she had been more or less wiped dry, too, although her underrobe was clinging to her body. The waist cord was untied. It surprised me to see how disheveled her hair was—it streamed down over her shoulders, and the neckband of her robe was soaking wet. When she had fainted before, at our house, her hair had always been tied up in a knot, never loose and flowing like this. I wondered if her appearance reflected Kimura's tastes.

He seemed to be quite at home, and had no trouble bringing me what I needed—washbowl, boiling water, and the rest. . . .

"We can't very well let her sleep here," I said, about an hour later.

"They go to bed early in the main house," he told me. "Madame Okada probably doesn't know what's happened."

But Ikuko's pulse was a good deal better, and I decided to take her home. I had Kimura call a taxi.

"I'll carry her out," he offered, stooping down so that I could lift her onto his back. I got her in position, still undressed, and then draped her kimono over her. We crossed the garden to the taxi; together we put her into it. The taxi was a very small one, and Kimura sat in front. All my wife's

clothing reeked of brandy; the air inside was sti-
fling. I sat holding her across my lap, and buried
my face in her damp, chilly hair; then I bent over
to kiss and caress her feet. I don't think Kimura
could see what was going on, but he may have
suspected it.

After we had carried her to the bedroom, he
said he hoped I wouldn't be suspicious about
what happened tonight. "Your daughter knows
everything," he added, and then asked if I needed
him any longer. I said I didn't.

As soon as he was gone I remembered that
Toshiko had come over ahead of us, and I went
to look for her. But she was gone too. Earlier,
when we carried Ikuko in from the taxi, she had
seemed to be waiting restlessly in the entrance
hall. Presumably she left without a word, just
after we arrived.

I came up to my study, and have quickly
jotted down all of the night's events—all that has
happened so far, that is. In the midst of writing, I
have savored the thought of the pleasures which
are to follow.

•

It was dawn before I fell asleep. Trying to decide the meaning of what happened last night has been an acute but frightening joy. I have yet to hear a word of explanation, whether from Kimura, Toshiko, or my wife. To be sure, I haven't had a chance to ask—but I haven't wanted to, quite so soon. I have found a kind of pleasure in thinking it over by myself, before hearing about it from anyone else. I allow my imagination to roam freely over all sorts of possibilities—discarding one for another, and then another—until, in the tightening grip of jealousy and rage, I feel myself quiver with a savage, irresistible lust. When the truth finally comes out, that pleasure will disappear.

Toward daybreak my wife began calling Kimura's name, in her usual delirious way. But this morning she repeated it over and over again, at intervals, now strongly and now weakly. At last, as her voice was rising once again, I took her.

In an instant my jealous rage had vanished. I no longer cared whether she was asleep or awake, shamming or not; I didn't even want to distinguish myself from Kimura. At that moment I felt I had burst into another world, soared up to some towering height, to the very zenith of ecstasy. This was reality, the past was only illusion. We were alone together, embracing. . . . Perhaps it would kill me, but the moment would last forever.

MARCH 19

· ·

I want to write down all I remember about last night. I knew my husband would be out, and I'd told him I might go along with Toshiko and Mr. Kimura to a movie. At half-past four Kimura-san arrived, but Toshiko didn't come until nearly five o'clock.

"Aren't you a little late?" I asked her.

"I'm afraid so," she said. "How about having dinner first? Mama, come and be my guest at Sekidencho. You haven't paid me a real visit yet, you know. And tonight I've got a pound of boned chicken!" She was carrying an armful of vegetables, too. As she shepherded us out she picked up the bottle of Courvoisier, which was still quite full, and said: "I'll let you donate this!" When I told her we shouldn't drink it in Papa's absence, she replied that her dinner wouldn't be complete without it.

"I don't want a full-course dinner," I said. "Let's keep it simple, since we're going to the movies afterward."

But she insisted that nothing was simpler than sukiyaki.

We put two little tables together in front of the piano, borrowed a gas burner from the main house, and started cooking at once. I was surprised to see that Toshiko had bought so much food, and in such variety. Not only the usual ingredients—onions, vermicelli, fresh bean curd—but Chinese cabbage, wheat-gluten cake, toasted bean curd, lily bulbs, and such. Instead of bringing them all out together, she added them little by little, one after another, as the supply diminished. There seemed to be more than a pound of chicken, too. Naturally, we didn't get around to the rice, but kept on drinking brandy.

"It's quite a novelty for your daughter to be acting as bartender, isn't it?" Kimura-san remarked. He seemed to be drinking more than usual.

After waiting until it was too late, Toshiko said: "I'm afraid we've missed the last show." But I no longer cared. I didn't think I was becoming really intoxicated, though. It's always that way with me—I suppress the effects of liquor perfectly well, up to a certain point. Then all of a sudden I lose control. Last night I intended to be cautious, thinking Toshiko might want to get me drunk. Yet I can't deny that at the same time I felt a kind of anticipation—or hope. Maybe the two of them planned it all in advance. But they wouldn't have been likely to admit it, so I didn't ask.

Once, though, Kimura-san said: "Do you think you ought to drink this much when your husband isn't here?" But he's getting to be a much better drinker himself, and he kept up with me glass for glass. I suppose we had the same thing in mind. As for me, I felt that I was only doing what my husband would have wished, since making him jealous seems to make him happy. I'm not saying my sole object was to please him, only that the thought of it gave me such a feeling of reas-

83

THE KEY

surance that I found myself drinking on and on.

There's something else I want to set down plainly today. I won't go so far as to say I love Kimura-san, but the truth is, I find him very attractive. I think I could even love him, if I tried. Of course that's because I've almost let myself be seduced, in order to make my husband jealous— but I'm sure I wouldn't have done it if I hadn't liked him. Up till now I've drawn a line, and I've been careful not to go beyond it. Now, though, I have a feeling that it's quite possible I might make a false step. I hope my husband won't put *too* much confidence in my faithfulness. I've endured everything for his sake, at his desire, but I'm beginning to lose confidence in myself. I don't know what will come of all this.

Still, I must admit I was curious to see Kimura-san in the nude. I wanted to see for myself, without any interference from my husband, that naked body I'd always dreamed of—was it really Kimura-san's? Suddenly I began to feel tipsy, and went to hide in the lavatory. Toshiko called to me through the door: "Mama, the bath is ready. Why don't you go in?"

Somewhere in my hazy mind I knew I would faint, knew that the person to come for me would

84

be Kimura-san. I can recall hearing Toshiko urge me once or twice more. Before long I made my way to the bath, opened the glass door, and went in and took off my clothes. I don't remember anything after that.

MARCH 24

•

Again last night my wife fainted at the Sekiden-cho house. She had gone out with Toshiko and Kimura after dinner, presumably to the movies; when they weren't back by eleven, I began to feel suspicious. I thought of telephoning, but that seemed absurd—I knew I would hear from them before long. As I waited, I became more and more impatient. I was trembling with annoyance—and with excitement.

A little past midnight Toshiko appeared, alone. She left her taxi waiting while she came in to tell me what had happened. After the movie—according to her story—Kimura insisted on seeing both of them home. They went first to Sekiden-cho, and stopped in for tea. Noticing that there

85

was still a good deal of brandy left, Toshiko added a spoonful of it to each of the cups. Soon Kimura and her mother were having a bit more; they finally emptied the bottle. Once again, the bath happened to be ready. One thing led to another just as it had a few nights before—so Toshiko said. It hardly amounted to an explanation.

"Did you leave them there alone?" I asked.

She nodded. "The phone isn't in yet, and I didn't like to call from the main house. Besides," she went on, "I knew you'd need a cab yourself, so I found one and came." She was looking hard at me, in her malicious way. "We were lucky the other night—it isn't easy to get a cab at this hour. I waited in front of the house for a while, but there just weren't any. Finally I walked over to the cab stand by the river, and found one of the drivers asleep there. I woke him up and had him bring me." Then she added, as if to herself: "I must have left the cottage about half an hour ago."

I guessed what was in her mind, but I merely thanked her for coming and asked her to look after the house. I collected everything I needed, and went to the taxi. Of course I didn't know how far the three of them had planned this together;

86

still, I could easily imagine that Toshiko had in-
stigated it. No doubt she had purposely left her
mother alone with Kimura for the half-hour—had
it been, perhaps, an hour?—that she managed to
spend in coming after me. I tried not to think
about what might have gone on during that inter-
val.

When I arrived, I found Ikuko lying there in
her underrobe, just as she was the other night.
Again her clothes were hanging along the wall.
Kimura brought hot water and a washbowl. She
seemed to be unconscious, even drunker than the
time before. However, I could see through her
pretense. It was obvious that she was only acting.
Her pulse was fairly strong, too. Since it would
have been pointless to give her a camphor injection, I decided to simulate it, and give her vitamins instead. Kimura noticed what I was doing,
and asked me, in a low voice, if vitamins would
be enough.

"Yes, I think so," I said calmly. "She doesn't
seem so bad tonight." And I proceeded with the
injection.

Later, Ikuko called Kimura's name over and
over again. Her voice had a new and ardent tone
—not the somewhat delirious one I was used to,

87

but a strong, piercing, imploring quality. As she approached a climax her cries became still more intense. Suddenly I felt the tip of my tongue being bitten—then the lobe of my ear. She had never been like this before.

When I think that it was Kimura who, overnight, turned her into such a bold, aggressive woman, I feel violently jealous, and at the same time grateful. Perhaps I should also be grateful to Toshiko. Ironically enough, she seems to be quite unaware of my curious state of mind. She doesn't know that by trying to hurt me she actually gives me pleasure.

Early this morning, after intercourse, I felt an awful giddiness. Ikuko's face, neck, shoulders, arms—the entire outline of her figure seemed double. It looked as if another and identical body overlapped her own. I must have fallen asleep shortly after that, but even in my dreams that double image persisted. At first her whole body was doubled; soon the various parts were scattered in space. Two pairs of eyes and two noses in a single row, two pairs of lips above them, and so on, all in the most vivid colors. The surrounding space was sky blue, the hair black, the lips crimson, the noses pure white—and that black,

88

that red, that white were far more brilliant than her actual coloring. They were as poisonously garish as a movie billboard.

In my dream, it occurred to me that seeing such vivid colors must be evidence of serious neurasthenia. Yet I kept on dreaming. Two pairs of feet—their skin was exquisitely fair—seemed to be floating under water. Unmistakably, they were *her* feet. Their soles floated separately, alongside. Just then a large white mass loomed up before me, like a bank of clouds; it was a shape I had once photographed—her buttocks, turned full toward me.

Hours later I had a different dream. Kimura was standing before me, naked; sometimes his head was transformed into mine, sometimes both our heads grew from a single body. The entire image was doubled.

MARCH 26

• •

For the third time now I've seen Kimura-san without my husband. Last night there was a new bottle of Courvoisier, still unopened, sitting in the alcove. "Did you bring this?" I asked Toshiko; but she denied it, saying she had no idea where it came from.

"The bottle was there when I got home yesterday," she went on. "I thought Mr. Kimura might have brought it."

"I don't know anything about it either," Kimura-san said. "It must have been your husband. I'm sure that's the answer. He's playing an elaborate joke on us."

"If it's Papa, he's being awfully sarcastic, isn't he?"

That's the way they talked about it. It does seem likely that he put the bottle there, but I really don't know what to think. I can't be sure Toshiko or Kimura-san didn't bring it.

On Wednesdays and Fridays Madame Okada goes to Osaka to teach and doesn't come home till eleven. The other night, after we began drinking, Toshiko slipped off to the main house. (It's the first time I've mentioned this. I've been afraid my husband would misunderstand, but there doesn't seem to be any further need to withhold the truth.) Again last night she disappeared early; even when Madame Okada came home she stayed on talking with her for quite a long while.

And again I fainted. Still, no matter what my condition was, I think I managed to hold that last line of resistance. I haven't yet had the courage to cross it, and I believe Kimura-san feels the same.

"I'm the one who lent your husband the Polaroid camera," he told me. "I did it because I knew he liked to get you drunk and look at you in the nude. But he couldn't be satisfied with the Polaroid, so he finally began taking pictures with a Zeiss Ikon. I suppose he wanted to search out every detail of your body—but more than that, I think he wanted to make me suffer. I think he likes having *me* develop the films; he likes exciting me, and making me fight a terrible temptation. And he relishes the thought that my own feelings are reflected in you, till you're as tormented as I am. It's cruel of him to do this to us, but I still don't want to betray him. I see how you are suffering, and I want to suffer with you—I want to suffer more and more deeply."

"Toshiko found those photographs in the French book she borrowed from you," I told him. "She said there must be some reason for it—they couldn't have been put there accidentally. What did you mean by that?"

"I hoped she might take some action if I

showed them to her," he answered. "I've never suggested anything in particular. It's just that, knowing there's a touch of Iago in her, I rather expected what happened on the night of the eighteenth—and the night of the twenty-third, and this evening too. Your daughter always took the initiative. I only kept quiet and followed her lead."

"This is the first time I've talked about our relationship," I said. "I've never discussed it before, not even with my husband. He seems to avoid asking about you. Maybe he's afraid to, and still tries to believe I've been faithful to him. I'd like to think so too, but I wonder if I really have been. You're the only person who can tell me that."

"Yes, of course you have," Kimura-san said. "There's one part of your body I've never touched. He wanted me a paper-thin distance from you, and so I've obeyed his wish. I've come as close as I could without violating that rule."

"Oh, I'm so glad to hear that!" I exclaimed. "You can't imagine how grateful I am!"

Kimura-san tells me I hate my husband, but the truth is, though I *do* hate him, I love him too. The more I hate him, the more passionate my love becomes. He puts someone like you, Kimura-san, between us, and if he didn't torture you his own passion wouldn't flare up—yet when I think that his aim, after all, is to give me pleasure, I simply can't turn against him. But couldn't you look at it as I do? He is identified with you, you are part of him, the two of you really one.

MARCH 28

•

I have had a retinal examination at the university eye clinic. I didn't want to, but Dr. Noma was so insistent that I finally took his advice.

They say that my dizziness comes from hardening of the cerebral arteries. The brain is congested, which causes dizziness, double vision, perhaps a partial blacking-out of consciousness. In severe cases there may be complete unconsciousness. I was asked if I didn't feel especially dizzy when I have to get up in the middle of the night, when I make a hasty movement or a sudden turn; and I had to admit that I did. They say that losing one's sense of equilibrium—feeling as if one were about to fall, or sink into the ground—results from an impairment of circulation in the inner ear.

Dr. Noma examined me, too, at the internal-medicine department. Today, besides taking my blood pressure, he made an electrocardiagram and a kidney examination.

"I'm surprised that your blood pressure is so high," Dr. Noma told me. "You'll have to be careful." I asked him how high it was, but he seemed reluctant to answer. "Both readings are around two hundred," he said at last. "The worst thing is that there's such a small difference between them. Instead of dosing yourself with hormones and stimulants, you ought to take something to lower your blood pressure. I'm afraid you'll have to abstain from sexual activity, and give up alcohol too. Stay away from salty foods and stimulants of any kind." Then he prescribed various drugs—Rutin C, Serpasil, Kallikrein—and said that I should be sure to have my blood pressure checked frequently from now on.

I am writing all this in my diary, with complete frankness, in order to see what effect it will have on Ikuko. For the present I intend to ignore the doctor's warning. If there is to be any change in our behavior, the first move will have to come from her. But I expect her to pretend that she hasn't read this, and to go on being as lustful as ever. That is her nature, she can hardly help it. By now I myself am no longer able to turn back. Now too, after the other night, she has suddenly become aggressive in searching for new and varied pleasures. It is her force that drives us on. As usual, though, she never utters a word during the act. Silently, by her movements, she expresses all her erotic feelings. Since she invariably pretends to be half asleep, there is no need to dim the light. I am captivated by her drunken, sleepy, yet deliciously shamefaced manner.

At first I kept my wife at a considerable distance from Kimura. However, as the stimulation gradually wore off I began to reduce that distance. The more I reduced it, the more jealous I became —and the more pleasure I derived. My plan was a great success. But, because Ikuko and I both want the same thing, we haven't known where to stop. It is almost three months since the New Year, and I cannot help marveling that I have dared to struggle so long to cope with her. Now indeed she must realize how much I love her. But what lies ahead? How can I continue to whip up my passion? At this rate the stimulation will soon wear off again—I have already put them in a situation that, under ordinary circumstances, would have to be called adultery. Yet even now I trust her. What possible way is left to bring them closer, without forcing her to be unfaithful? I must try to think of one, although they—with Toshiko's help —will probably hit on something before I do.

I have said that Ikuko is secretive, but so am I. It's no wonder that Toshiko, taking after her parents, is secretive too. But Kimura is even worse. How extraordinary that the lives of four such sly, secretive persons should be intertwined. More extraordinary still, the four of us—all the while deceiving one another—are co-operating quite effectively. That is, each of us seems to have his own scheme in mind, but in fact we all have a single aim. We are doing our best to corrupt Ikuko.

MARCH 30

••

This afternoon Toshiko came over, and persuaded me to go along on a little trip to Arashiyama. Kimura-san—it's vacation time just now—was waiting for us at the Omiya streetcar terminal; we went on together from there. It seems that it was all Toshiko's idea. I felt very grateful to her.

We strolled along the bank of the river, took a boat as far as the Rankyo Hotel, then, after resting a bit near the bridge, went to look at the garden of the Tenryuji Temple. For the first time in ages I was breathing fresh, healthy air. I think I'd like to go on an outing of this kind more often. It's too bad my husband is such a bookworm.

Toward evening we started back. We left the streetcar at Hyakumamben and went our separate ways. The day had been so exhilarating that for once I didn't feel like drinking brandy.

MARCH 31

• •

Last night my husband and I went to bed cold sober. Around midnight I let him see the toes of my left foot, exposing them beyond the edge of the blanket, out into the glare of the fluorescent lamp. He was quick to notice, and got into my

97

bed. Then, bathed in that strong light and not in the least intoxicated, we made love. An astonishing performance. I could see that he was flushed with excitement.

Because of the vacation, he's usually home all day (and so is Madame Okada). Of course he goes out walking; he wanders about the neighborhood for an hour or two, and then comes home. He likes to walk, but I think he also likes to give me time to read his diary. Whenever he says: "I'll be back soon," I feel as if I've been told: "Be sure to read my diary!" That makes me all the more determined not to. But maybe, under the circumstances, I ought to give him a chance to read my own.

MARCH 31

•

Last night Ikuko amazed and delighted me. She didn't pretend to be drunk or even ask me to put out the light. After displaying herself in a most provocative manner, she deliberately set to work arousing me. I was surprised to find her so expert at the art of love. In time I suppose I'll understand the meaning of this.

The dizziness has been so bad that I began worrying, after all, and went to Dr. Kodama to have him check my blood pressure. I could see that it alarmed him. He said it was almost high enough to break his instrument. According to him, I need absolute rest—I ought to stop work at once.

APRIL 1

• •

Today Toshiko brought over a Miss Kawai, who teaches dressmaking, and who also makes things to order. There's no tax, so she can do it for twenty or thirty per cent less than the usual prices. Toshiko gets all her clothes from her. Except for my school uniforms, I've never worn Western clothing—my tastes are old-fashioned, and kimonos are becoming to my figure. But although I have no intention of changing styles at my age, I let Toshiko persuade me to order a dress from her. I know I can't keep it a secret, but I felt embarrassed and asked her to come this afternoon, while

99

my husband was away. I had Toshiko and Miss Kawai pick out the fabric and the pattern. I said I'd like the skirt long—at least two inches below the knee—since my legs are a little bowed. Miss Kawai told me they couldn't really be called bowed—even Westerners' legs were often curved that much.

They showed me all sorts of samples, and pointed out a pattern in *Modes et travaux*, a gray and russet tweed ensemble. Both of them said I should try it, so I agreed. It seems it won't cost over ten thousand yen, but I'll have to buy shoes too, and a few accessories.

APRIL 2

• •

Went out this afternoon. Back by evening.

APRIL 3

• •

Went out at ten. Bought shoes at a shop on Kawaramachi. Back by evening.

APRIL 4

· ·

Went out this afternoon. Back by evening.

APRIL 5

· ·

Went out this afternoon. Back by evening.

APRIL 5

·

Ikuko's routine has changed. She goes out almost every afternoon—sometimes even in the morning —and comes home four or five hours later, in time for dinner. The two of us have dinner together. She usually won't drink—brandy doesn't seem to appeal to her any more. Perhaps the fact that Kimura is free just now has something to do with her new habits. I have no idea where she goes.

At two o'clock this afternoon Toshiko turned

up unexpectedly, and asked: "Where's Mama?"

"She's always out around this time," I said. "Isn't she at your place?"

"I haven't seen anything of her," Toshiko replied, tilting her head doubtfully; "or of Mr. Kimura, either. Where do you suppose she goes?"

But I suspect that Toshiko herself is in on the secret.

APRIL 6

• •

Went out this afternoon. Back by evening.

Lately I've been going out every day. My husband is usually here when I leave. He's shut up in his study, sitting crouched over his desk with an open book in front of him, as if he's absorbed in reading. I don't think he is, though. I imagine he's far too busy wondering what I do in the hours I spend away from home. Of course there's no doubt that while I'm gone he comes down to the sitting room, takes my diary out of the cabinet, and reads it. But unfortunately he finds it doesn't tell him anything—I've purposely been vague about my activities of the past few days.

Before leaving I go up to his study, open the sliding door a crack, and call in to say I'll be gone for a while. Then I steal down the stairs as if I were making an escape. Sometimes I only call from the stairs. He never turns to look at me; either he nods and murmurs "All right," or he doesn't answer.

I need scarcely say I don't go out just to let him read my diary. I've been meeting Kimura-san at a certain rendezvous. I go because I've wanted to lie in his arms—somewhere flooded by the healthy rays of the sun, at a time when my mind isn't dulled by liquor. It's true that I've been alone with him at Toshiko's place, away from my husband, but I've always been hopelessly drunk at the moment when our bodies touch. On January thirtieth I wrote about wondering "how much truth there was in my dream of Kimura-san" and, on March nineteenth, about being curious "to see for myself, without any interference from my husband, that naked body I'd always dreamed of." Those feelings, still unsatisfied, lurked in my heart. Whatever the cost, I wanted to gaze long and deep—fully conscious, and in broad daylight

—at the man I knew to be the genuine, palpable Kimura-san, not just a phantom brought to me through my husband.

Joyfully, but with an eerie sense of having done this before, I discovered that Kimura-san, in the flesh, was the very man I've dreamed of sleeping with so many times since early this year. Once I wrote about "grasping his strong young arms," of being "pressed tight against his firm, resilient body"—above all, of being startled by his dazzlingly fair skin. Now I've actually seen him, and know what he's like. At last, beyond the shadow of a doubt, I have grasped his young arms, felt my breasts tight against his firm body, felt the warm, silky touch of his white skin.

But how strange that my illusions mirrored reality! I can't think it's only a coincidence that my dream-image of Kimura-san corresponded so perfectly to the real man. I feel as if I'd known him from a former life, as if he had a mysterious power to haunt my dreams.

Now that his image has unmistakably come alive, I can separate him completely from my husband. Once and for all, I hereby strike out the words "you are part of him, the two of you really one." The only resemblance between them

104

is that they both appear to be slightly built. In the nude Kimura-san looks very different. His chest is surprisingly deep and his whole body radiates vitality; he's not at all like my scrawny husband, with his bad complexion, his slack, sagging skin. There's a glossy sheen and freshness to Kimura-san's skin, a tinge of pink under the white, whereas my husband's dark, sallow skin seems dead; its waxy smoothness still nauseates me. My feelings about my husband used to be divided equally between love and hate, but the balance is tipping more and more toward hate. How many times a day I sigh to think what a miserable sort of man I married: if only Kimura-san were in his place!

Yet if I say that, having come this far, I still haven't crossed that last line—will my husband believe me? Whether he does or not, it's the truth. Of course I'm interpreting the "last line" in an exceedingly narrow sense; maybe I should say I've done everything *but* violate it. I was brought up by conventional-minded parents, and I can't escape their rigid way of thinking. Somehow I have the notion that, no matter what happens, as long as I don't engage in what my husband likes to call "orthodox" sexual intercourse, I haven't

really been unfaithful. And so I've remained faithful to him, in that sense, but I don't stop at anything that isn't covered by that strict definition.
I'd prefer not to be specific, though.

APRIL 8

•

This afternoon I almost ran into Ikuko. I was going west on Shijo, several blocks past the Fujii
Department Store, when I happened to see her
leave a shop thirty or forty feet ahead. However,
she turned and went the other way. I looked at
my watch: it was half-past four. To judge from
the time, she should have been going east, toward
home; I suppose she saw me coming and was trying to avoid me. She must have been startled,
since I seldom venture out of the Higashiyama
district. I hardly ever go downtown.

Quickening my pace a little, I caught up to
within a few yards of her. But I didn't call, nor
did she look back. We both kept on walking, the
same distance apart. Meanwhile, I had glanced in
at the window of the shop she had just left, a win-

dow full of ladies' accessories—lace and nylon gloves, all kinds of earrings, pendants, and the like. It occurred to me that she never wore Western clothes and wouldn't have any use for such things—but then I noticed, to my surprise, that pearl earrings were dangling from her ears.

When had she acquired a taste for wearing earrings with kimono? Had she just bought them and put them on in the shop, or was she in the habit of wearing them whenever she was out of my sight? Now and then, during the past month, I have seen her in one of those fashionable short *haori* called tea-jackets. And she had it on today. Before, she always refused to take up the latest styles, but I had to admit that this one was not unbecoming to her. What surprised me even more was that the earrings suited her so well. I recalled something Akutagawa Ryunosuke once wrote about the alluring pallor of the back of a Chinese woman's ears. My own wife's ears, seen from the back, were like that. They enhanced the pearls, and were enhanced by them—the effect was quite lovely. But I couldn't believe that this was her own idea. As usual, I had mixed feelings of jealousy and gratitude. It was chagrining to think that someone else had discovered this exotic aspect of her beauty, which I had failed to see. I suppose husbands are not so observant, because they look at their wives in a fixed way.

She crossed Karasumaru Avenue, and kept straight on. Besides her handbag, she was carrying a long, narrow parcel, probably from the shop she had just left. I couldn't tell what was in it. When I saw her going on down the next block I crossed the street and walked rapidly ahead, to let her know that I wasn't following her any more. Then I got on an east-bound streetcar at Horikawa.

She came home about an hour after me. The earrings were gone—in her bag, presumably. She was still carrying the parcel, but she didn't open it in my presence.

APRIL 10

• •

I wonder if my husband's diary reveals anything about the state of his health. How much does it worry him? I have no way of finding out what he's thinking, of course, but for at least a month I've noticed that there's something wrong. Lately

108

his complexion has been worse than ever—really ashen. He often falters going up and down the stairs. He has always had a strong memory, but he's becoming terribly forgetful; sometimes, talking on the phone, he can't think of a person's name, and he seems bewildered. When he's walking around the house he sometimes stops short and closes his eyes, or holds fast to a pillar.

Although he writes all his letters on formal letter paper, by brush, his writing is becoming dreadfully clumsy. (You'd expect a man's calligraphy to improve with age.) Frequently he's even wrong. I only see what is on the envelopes, but there's always a mistake or two. And the mistakes are glaring ones: he may give the wrong date, by several months, or put down something absurd for our own street number. Once he wrote "June" for "April," then crossed that out and neatly corrected it to "August." Worst of all, a letter to his uncle had two errors in the name itself. With dates and addresses, I quietly correct them before mailing; but this time I didn't know how to fix it, so I warned him, casually, that the name was wrong. He was obviously perturbed, but tried to seem calm. "So it is," he said, and put the letter on his desk without immediately correcting it. It's all very well about the envelopes, since I look them over carefully, but there's no telling what mistakes I'd find inside.

Maybe it's already common knowledge that he's behaving oddly. The other day I went to see Dr. Kodama—he's the only one I could consult about this—and asked him to persuade my husband to have a check-up. "That's something I've been wanting to talk to you about," he told me. It seems my husband himself was so worried that he went to see Dr. Noma, a professor on the medical-school faculty. Then, badly frightened by what he heard, he came to Dr. Kodama.

Dr. Kodama explained to me that, not being a specialist, he couldn't make a definite diagnosis. "Still," he went on, "I was shocked to see how high his blood pressure was."

"How high was it?" I asked.

He hesitated a moment. "Perhaps I shouldn't tell you this," he said. "When I tried to measure it, my instrument nearly broke. It went over the top of the scale, and kept on climbing. I had to stop. I can't say how high it is."

I asked if my husband knew.

"He's been warned by Dr. Noma before," he answered, "but hasn't listened. I told him

frankly that it was a dangerous condition." (I'm
writing this because I don't think it matters if he
reads it, since he's already heard it from Dr.
Kodama.)

I suppose I'm to blame for having
brought it on. If it hadn't been for my demands
on him, he wouldn't have sunk to such depravity.
When I talked to Dr. Kodama I had to blush.
Fortunately he doesn't know the truth about our
sexual relations. He seems to think I'm so passive
that my husband's excesses are entirely his own
fault. Probably my husband would say it all came
about because he wanted to give me pleasure. I
won't deny that; but for my part, I've done everything possible to fulfill my duty to him, I've put
up with things that were really hard to bear. Toshiko would call me "a model wife." In a way, I
think I am.

But there's no use trying to fix the blame,
now that it's too late. We enticed each other; we
urged each other on; we fought desperately, without quarter; and now at last, driven by an irresistible force, we've come to this.

I don't know whether I ought to mention it,
or what may happen if he reads this, but the
truth is, he isn't the only one whose health is bad.

I'm not much better off myself. I began to be aware of it in January. Years ago, of course, when Toshiko was about ten, I started coughing up traces of blood, and the doctor warned me that I was showing symptoms of tuberculosis. But since that had turned out to be a mild case, I didn't worry about these new symptoms. (Yes, and the first time, too, I ignored the doctor's advice. It's not that I wasn't afraid of dying, but my instinct wouldn't let me dwell on it. I shut my eyes to the terror of death, and yielded blindly to sexual impulse. Although he was shocked at such recklessness, my husband soon gave in to me. I suppose I'd have died then, if I'd been unlucky. Somehow, as rash as I was, I got over it.)

And so this year, late in January, I had a premonition of illness; every now and then I felt a warm, itching sensation in my chest. One day in February, just as before, I coughed up a scarlet-flecked bit of phlegm containing a thread of blood. There wasn't much, but it happened two or three times. At the moment it seems to have subsided; I don't know when it may begin again. I'm sure I have a fever—my body is heavy, and my face and hands feel hot—but I don't intend to take my temperature. (Once I did, and it was 99.7°.

I haven't taken it since.) I've also decided not to consult a doctor, though I've been having night sweats too.

Maybe this won't be any more serious than last time, but it's not the kind of thing you can make light of. Luckily, as my doctor once told me, I have a strong stomach. He said people with chest trouble usually get thin: it was amazing I didn't lose my appetite. What worries me most is that my chest often aches quite severely, and by afternoon I feel exhausted. (To resist that feeling I press all the closer to Kimura-san. I can't overcome it without him.) Before, my chest didn't ache so badly, and I didn't feel such fatigue. Perhaps I'm gradually getting worse—I can't believe that this is only a trivial matter. Besides, I've done everything to ruin my health. They say drinking aggravates this illness; if that's so, it'll be a miracle if I recover. Now that I think of it, maybe I've let myself get drunk so often because I've had a feeling of despair, a feeling that I haven't long to live, anyway.

•

I had thought that my wife might begin keeping different hours, which is exactly what she has done. Now that Kimura's vacation is over they can no longer meet in the afternoon. For a few days she stayed at home instead of going out immediately after lunch. However, yesterday at five o'clock Toshiko appeared, as if by previous arrangement, and Ikuko began getting ready to leave. I was in my study, but I soon realized what was happening.

A few minutes later she came upstairs and called to me through the door: "I'm leaving now, but I'll be home soon."

As usual, I merely said: "All right."

"Toshiko's here," she added, pausing on her way down. "You can have dinner with her."

"What about you?" I asked, somewhat annoyed.

"I'll eat when I get back," she said. "You can wait for me if you like."

But I told her not to hurry on my account. "I'll go ahead. You might as well have dinner out."

Suddenly I was curious to see what she was wearing. I got up quickly, went into the hall, and looked down the stairs. She had already reached the bottom, but I could see that she had on those pearl earrings. (Perhaps she would have put them on later if she had expected me to come out.) She was slipping on a pair of white lace gloves, too—I thought of the parcel she was carrying the other day. It seemed to embarrass her to be seen like this. Toshiko was just remarking how well the gloves suited her.

About half-past six Baya came to say that dinner was ready. When I went down I found Toshiko waiting.

"You needn't have stayed," I told her. "I can eat by myself, you know."

"Mama said I ought to spend a little more time with you," she said. I gathered that there was something she wanted to talk about.

It is true that I seldom have dinner alone with her, for of course Ikuko is usually here. Lately she's been going out a great deal, before dinner or after, but she makes a point of being home at dinnertime. Perhaps that is why I was feeling a certain loneliness, a sad, empty mood such as I have rarely experienced. And Toshiko's company only deepened my sense of loneliness; she was really being much too kind. Knowing her, I don't think it was accidental.

"Papa," she began, as we sat down at the table, "do you know where Mama goes?"

"I haven't the slightest idea," I said; "and I don't care to find out, either."

But she said flatly: "Osaka." Then she waited to see my reaction.

I almost blurted out "Osaka?"—but I stopped myself. "Is that so?" I said, as calmly as I could.

Toshiko went on to explain that the place she went to was five or six minutes' walk from the Kyobashi station, less than an hour from here by interurban express. "Shall I give you some more details?" she asked, and seemed quite ready to.

I tried to change the subject. "Never mind about that," I said. "How do you happen to know so much?"

"I helped find the place," she said coolly. "Mr. Kimura thought they'd be seen in Kyoto, and wondered if I knew of somewhere not too far away. So I asked a sophisticated friend of mine, the sort of girl who knows all about such things."

With that, she poured out a glass of brandy and offered it to me. I haven't been drinking recently, but she had brought the bottle of Courvoisier to the table. I took a sip, to hide my embarrassment.

"What do you think now, if I'm not being too inquisitive?" Toshiko said.

"Think about what?" I asked.

"Suppose Mama insists she still hasn't betrayed you," she said. "Would you believe that?" I asked whether her mother had told her anything like that.

"No, but I heard it from Mr. Kimura," she answered. "He says she's still being faithful to you—though I don't take that kind of nonsense seriously."

Toshiko poured another glassful. I accepted it without hesitation, and drank it down. I felt like getting drunk. "Do as you please," I said. "It's up to you whether you want to take it seriously or not."

"But how about *you?*" she asked.

"I trust Ikuko," I said. "No one has to defend her to me. Even if Kimura said he'd slept with her, I wouldn't believe it. She's not the kind to deceive me."

"Oh?" Toshiko gave a faint, muffled laugh.

117

THE KEY

"Still, even supposing he hasn't 'slept with her,' in the way you mean, there are nastier ways of satisfying—"

"Will you stop it?" I said sharply. "Don't be so impudent: you talk like a sophisticated bitch yourself! Go on home! I don't need you around here."

"I'm going!" she said, flinging down her rice bowl. And she left.

My agitation at being caught off guard by her took a long time to subside. When she said "Osaka" I felt as if I had been kicked in the stomach—and the feeling lasted. Yet that doesn't mean I have never guessed what was going on. Perhaps the real shock was being confronted with something that I had done my best to ignore.

Of course it was the first time I had heard that they were meeting in Osaka. But where? I wondered. A small hotel, perhaps a disreputable one? I couldn't keep from imagining what kind of place it was, what their room was like, how they looked together. . . . "Asked a sophisticated friend of mine"?—somehow I was reminded of a cheap, cramped, one-room apartment. I pictured them in a high, Western-style bed; strangely enough, I felt I *wanted* them that way, rather

118

than on the soft, matted floor of a purely Japanese room. "Some extremely unnatural method"—"other, nastier ways"—I could see them in all sorts of positions, a tangle of arms and legs. . . .

Doubts began to well up in me. Why had Toshiko made her disclosure? Had Ikuko suggested it? She may have written the same thing in her diary, and then become afraid that I wouldn't read it—or wouldn't admit I had. Perhaps she used Toshiko to force me to recognize that this time she had yielded herself completely. That was what worried me most. When Toshiko said: "I don't take that kind of nonsense seriously," hadn't Ikuko put the words into her mouth? Now that it's come to this, I realize how mistaken I was to reveal that "her physical endowment for it is equaled by very few women." I wonder how long she was able to resist the temptation to experiment with another man.

One reason why I haven't doubted her earlier is that she has never refused to sleep with me. Even when she has obviously just come from seeing him, she has never shown the slightest reluctance to let me make love to her. Far from it, she lures me on. I took this to mean that she wasn't sleeping with him. But I had overlooked

119

her innate sensuality. Unlike most women, Ikuko welcomes repeated love-making—and can keep it up day after day. For anyone else, surely, it would be unbearable to repeat the act with a hated partner after leaving one you love. Yet even if she wanted to refuse me, her body would respond willingly to my embrace.

It was nine o'clock last night when she came home. I went into the bedroom at eleven, and found her already in bed. She was incredibly ardent, so ardent that I was forced into the passive role. In warmth, in eagerness, in responsiveness, she left nothing to be desired. Her seductive attitudes, her bold technique, the way she led us, step by step, to the most ravishing pleasure—all this proved how she abandoned herself to love.

APRIL 15

•

I can see that my brain is steadily deteriorating. Since January, when I became intent on satisfying Ikuko, I have found myself losing interest in everything else. My ability to think has so declined that I can't concentrate for five minutes. My mind teems with sexual fantasies. For years I have been a voracious reader, whatever the circumstances, but now I spend the whole day without reading a word. And yet, out of long habit, I continue to sit at my desk. My eyes are fixed on a book, but I scarcely read at all. To be sure, I am suffering from a visual disturbance that makes reading extremely difficult. The print looks double, and I have to go over the same line again and again.

Now at last I have been bewitched into an animal that lives by night, an animal good only for mating. By day, when I am shut up in my study, I feel intolerably tired and bored; at the same time, I am a prey to terrible anxiety. Going out for a stroll is somewhat diverting, but my dizziness gives me trouble in walking. I feel as if I am about to fall over backward. Even if I go out, I don't venture far from home. Leaning on my cane, I hobble about Hyakumamben, Kurodani, the Eikan Temple; I stay away from busy streets, and spend most of the time resting on benches. My legs are so weak that I soon become exhausted.

When I came back today Ikuko was talking

to Miss Kawai, the dressmaker, in the sitting room. I was going to stop for a cup of tea, but she exclaimed: "Don't come in just now!" I peeped in anyway, and saw her trying on a foreign-style dress. She objected, and I went up to my study. Later I heard her calling to say that she would be gone for a little while. She seemed to be leaving with Miss Kawai.

From the second-floor window I looked at the two of them walking along together. It was the first time I had seen Ikuko in Western clothes. No doubt this is what she was getting ready for when she began wearing gloves and earrings with kimono. But, to tell the truth, her new dress is not very becoming. It doesn't seem to suit her. I should have thought that, compared with the squat, shapeless Miss Kawai, Ikuko would have looked attractive in such clothes. But Miss Kawai is accustomed to them, and wears them with a flair. My wife's earrings and lace gloves didn't suit her as well as they had before. Then they had seemed exotic, but today, with foreign dress, they struck me as unnatural, ill-assorted. There was a lack of harmony between her clothes, her accessories, and her figure.

These days it is becoming popular to wear

Japanese things in a Western manner, but Ikuko does the opposite. You can see that she is built for kimono. Her shoulders are too sloping for Western clothes. Worse yet, her legs are bowed—slender and trim enough, but excessively curved out from knee to ankle. In silk stockings her ankles seem rather puffy. Moreover, the way she carries herself—her walk, the movements of her shoulders and trunk, the way she holds her hands, the tilt of her head—everything about her is pliant and feminine in the traditional Japanese style, a style that is suited to kimono.

All the same, I felt a strange voluptuousness in her slender, supple figure, her awkwardly curved legs. This was something that had been concealed from me when she wore kimono. As I watched her walk away I gazed admiringly at the distorted beauty of her legs below the tweed skirt. And I thought of tonight.

APRIL 16

• •

This morning I went shopping, to the Nishiki Street market. For weeks now I've been out of the habit—I've left everything to Baya. But it seems unfair to my husband, somehow, as if I'm slighting my duty as a housewife. And so today I went. (It's true that I've scarcely had time for trips to Nishiki Street; I've been kept busy by a far more important matter.)

At the vegetable shop I always go to I bought garden peas, broad beans, and bamboo shoots. Seeing the bamboo shoots reminded me that the cherry-blossom season was over—gone before I'd even thought of it. Wasn't it last year that Toshiko and I went to look at the flowers together, walking along the canal from the Silver Pavilion to the Honen Temple? The blossoms along there must have fallen by now. But what a restless, uneasy spring this has been! The last two or three months have gone by in a twinkling, like a dream.

I was home by eleven, and went upstairs to change the flowers in the study, to put in some mimosa that Madame Okada sent over from her garden today. Apparently my husband had slept late; he came in while I was arranging the mimosa. He's always been an early riser, until quite recently.

"Did you just get up?" I said.

He asked if it was Saturday, and then: "I suppose you'll be out all day tomorrow." His voice sounded drowsy, as if he were still half asleep. (But I could tell that he was worried.) I murmured a vague reply.

About two o'clock I heard someone at the door, and found a man I didn't know standing there. He said he was a massage therapist from the Ishizuka Clinic. It seemed most unlikely that anyone at our house would have called such a person, but Baya came up and said she'd sent for him on my husband's orders. That was very odd. He's always disliked the notion of being touched by a stranger; this is the first time he's ever let a masseur near him. Baya said he'd been complaining that his shoulders were so stiff he could hardly turn his head, and she told him she knew a wonderful massage doctor. Wouldn't he just try him? It was like magic—after once or twice, he'd forget he'd ever had such troubles. He seemed to be in a great deal of pain, and asked her to send for him.

The man was about fifty, rather sinister-looking, thin, wearing dark glasses. I thought he might be blind, but he wasn't. Baya was upset when I referred to him as a masseur. "He'll get angry if you call him that," she said. "He's a doctor!"

As soon as he was in our bedroom the "doctor" had my husband lie down, and climbed on the bed himself to perform his treatment. He was wearing a clean white clinic coat, but he gave the impression of being dirty. I didn't like to see him there on the bed—I think it's quite natural to have an aversion to masseurs. And this one kept saying: "Pretty stiff, aren't you? I'll have those kinks out in no time!" He had a ridiculously self-important air.

After massaging my husband till four o'clock, he said: "You'll feel fine after another session or two. I'll be back tomorrow." Then he left.

"How do you feel?" I asked my husband.

"A little better," he said, "but it was quite an ordeal. My whole body aches from the pounding and squeezing."

I reminded him that the man would be back tomorrow.

"Well, let him try it once or twice more," he said. He did seem awfully stiff.

"I suppose you'll be out all day tomorrow," he remarked again. It was hard for me to tell him:

"I'm going out now, too," but it couldn't be helped.

At half-past four I changed into my new Western clothes, put on my earrings, and deliberately looked in at the bedroom, as much as to say: "I'm leaving."

"Are you going for a walk?" I asked him, to hide my embarrassment.

"Yes, I'll be leaving too," he said, lying there flat on his back, still worn out from the treatment.

APRIL 17

••

A day so critical for my husband is critical for me, too. Maybe what I write here will preserve the memory of it for the rest of my life. I'd like to put down all that's happened, minutely, concealing nothing. Still, it's best not to be too hasty. At this point I'd be wise to avoid going into detail about where and how I've spent my time.

Anyway, my Sunday plans were made long

in advance, and I carried them out exactly as I'd intended. As usual I went to meet Kimura at our hotel in Osaka, and enjoyed a few hours of happiness with him. Today we were ecstatically happy, perhaps more than any of our other Sundays together. We made love in every conceivable way. I did whatever he wanted, yielding myself completely to him. I twisted my body into fantastic postures that would have seemed unthinkable with my husband. When on earth had I acquired such skill, such freedom? I couldn't help being astonished, though I knew I owed it all to Kimura.

Always, when we meet there, we abandon ourselves to love; we regret even the slightest pause, and never waste a moment in idle talk. But today Kimura suddenly fixed a sharp look on me, and asked: "What are you thinking, Ikuko?" (He's been calling me Ikuko for some time now.)

"Nothing," I said. But just then—an experience I'd never had at a time like that—my husband's face flashed into my mind. I couldn't imagine why.

As I was trying to erase that image, Kimura said: "It's your husband, isn't it? I seem to be worrying about him too." He went on to say how awkward he felt about visiting our house, though he really ought to call on us soon. In fact, he'd written home and asked them to send us some more mullet roe—hadn't it reached us yet?

That was all we said, and once again we plunged into our world of love. But now I wonder if I'd had a kind of premonition.

When I came home at five, my husband was out. The massage doctor had called again, Baya said, and had treated him at least half an hour longer than yesterday. She reported what the man had told him: the stiffness in his shoulders was a sign of high blood pressure, but doctors' medicines wouldn't do any good, not even from one of those fancy medical-school doctors. "You'd better leave it to me," he had said. "I'll guarantee to cure you. I'm not just a physical therapist, I use acupuncture and moxa, too. If massage doesn't work, I'll use the needles: it'll help your dizziness within a day. Even though your blood pressure *is* high, you shouldn't worry about having it measured all the time. As long as you do, it'll keep going higher and higher. Lots of people get along perfectly well at two hundred, or at two hundred and forty or fifty, without taking any special care of themselves. It's best not to worry. A little alcohol and tobacco won't do any harm. You'll get over it," he had reassured him. "Your high blood pressure is definitely not going to kill you."

According to Baya, my husband was quite taken with the man. He told him to come every day, for the time being, and said he'd stop going to the doctor.

At six thirty he came back from his walk, and at seven we had dinner together. Baya cooked the things I bought at Nishiki Street yesterday; we had broad beans, garden peas with Koya bean curd, soup made out of the bamboo shoots. In addition, there was about a half-pound of tenderloin of beef. He's supposed to be on a vegetarian diet, but to cope with me he eats beef every day. Sukiyaki, grilled meats, roasts, all sorts of dishes —what he likes most is half-raw steak, dripping with blood. He seems to feel uneasy if he doesn't have it. I usually broil the steaks myself when I'm home, since they're hard to time.

I could see that the mullet roe had arrived; there was some on the table. Soon my husband suggested having a drink to go with it, and brought over the Courvoisier. But we didn't drink very much. The other day when he quarreled with Toshiko he nearly emptied the bottle; we finished off what was left with a glass apiece. Then he went back upstairs. At ten thirty I told him the bath was ready. After he finished, I bathed—the second time today. I'd had a bath in Osaka, but took another for appearance' sake. That's happened before.

When I came into our room I found my husband already in bed. As soon as he saw me he turned on the floor lamp. Nowadays he likes to keep the bedroom dim, except when we're making love. Hardening of the arteries seems to be affecting his sight: he's bothered by flickering double and triple vision. Sometimes the strain is so bad he has to shut his eyes. That's why he turns the fluorescent lamp on full only at that special time. Now it has a stronger bulb, so it's quite powerful.

When he looked at me in that sudden glare of light, he blinked with astonishment. After bathing, I had put on my earrings. I got into bed, purposely lying so that he could see my jeweled ears. As trivial a thing as that, the merest novelty, is enough to arouse him. He calls me sex-mad, but I'm sure there's no other man so obsessed by it. From morning till night it's his one concern. He never fails to respond to the slightest hint; whenever he sees a chance, he takes advantage of it.

In a moment he was climbing into my bed, embracing me, showering kisses on my ears. I lay there with tight-shut eyes, letting him do as he pleased. And that sensation—being titillated by a "husband" I can no longer say I love—was not wholly unpleasant. Even while I was thinking how clumsy his kisses were, compared with Kimura's, the queer, ticklish sensation from his tongue didn't seem merely disagreeable. It *was* disagreeable; but it had a kind of sweetness, too, and I was able to enjoy its flavor. It's true I detest that man from the bottom of my heart; yet when I think how infatuated he is with me, I have an urge to drive him into paroxysms of desire. I'm a person who can keep love and lust completely separate. On the one hand, I treat him coldly, find him nauseating, even; on the other, I'm so eager to seduce him that before I know it I've seduced myself. At first I'm icily calm, absorbed in wondering how I can excite him further. Maliciously I watch him gasp as if he's losing his mind, and I'm intoxicated by the skill of my own technique. But then at last I find myself gasping the same way, as excited as he is.

Tonight I repeated with him, one after another, all the things I'd done with Kimura this afternoon. How very different it was—I began to feel sorry for my clumsy husband. Yet somehow, as this was going through my mind, I became just as aroused as I'd been in the afternoon. I locked my arms around him, embracing him as fiercely as I'd embraced Kimura. (I suppose he would say this proves how oversexed I am.) Again and again I clasped him, until I was on the verge of a climax. At that moment his body began to quiver; then he went limp, and collapsed heavily on me.

I knew instantly that this was serious. When I spoke to him, he only uttered a hollow, meaningless sound. I felt a warm liquid on my cheek—his mouth was open, and saliva was dribbling from it.

APRIL 18

• •

I remembered what Dr. Kodama told me to do in case of an emergency like this. Gently, laboriously,

I began to pull myself out from under that inert body. (He was settling forward, as if borne down by a crushing weight. Doing my best not to jolt him, I drew my head free. First, though, I took off his glasses. That blank face of his—eyes half opened, muscles slack—had never been more repulsive.) I got out of bed and slowly, with great care, turned him on his back. Then I propped his head up with pillows. He was stark naked (so was I, except for my earrings); but since I knew he needed absolute quiet, all I did was to lay his night kimono over him.

The whole left side of his body seemed to be paralyzed. I looked to see what time it was: three minutes past one. It occurred to me to turn off the fluorescent lamp and use only the little night lamp, with a cloth to shade it. I telephoned Toshiko and Dr. Kodama, and asked them to come right away; I told Toshiko to wake the iceman and bring along fifteen pounds of ice. Although I meant to be very calm, the receiver trembled in my hand.

Toshiko got here about forty minutes later. I was in the kitchen looking for an ice bag; she came in, put the ice on the drainboard, and glanced sharply at me to see my expression. Then she turned away, casually, and began cracking the ice. I explained Papa's condition to her. She showed no emotion whatever, only nodding occasionally as if to say there was no use getting alarmed. After that we went to the bedroom and applied the ice bag to the side that wasn't paralyzed. We didn't exchange a single unnecessary word. We didn't even look at each other. . . . We tried not to look.

At two o'clock Dr. Kodama arrived. I had Toshiko stay at the bedside, and went to meet him. On our way to the room I hastily explained the circumstances of my husband's stroke—including something I hadn't mentioned to Toshiko. Once again I blushed.

Dr. Kodama's examination was very thorough. He asked for a flashlight, and used it to test the patient's eye reflexes. Then he wanted a chopstick. Toshiko brought a pair from the kitchen. "Now make the room a little brighter," he said, and had us turn on the fluorescent lamp. He rubbed the tip of a chopstick up the soles of the feet slowly, from heel to toe, repeating this several times. That was for Babinski's reflex, he told me later. When one of the feet reacts by bending back, it indicates that there has been a cerebral hemorrhage on the other side. In this case, he had to conclude that part of the brain had been cut off, somewhere on the right side.

Next he took off the light blanket I'd covered my husband with and rolled his night kimono up as far as his abdomen. For the first time Dr. Kodama and Toshiko realized that my husband had been naked. They both seemed to shrink from the sight of him—stretched out under that ugly glare. I felt more embarrassed than ever. It was hard to believe that only an hour ago that man had been lying with me. As often as he's looked at me in the nude, even photographed me, I had never looked at him this way before. Of course I could have if I'd wanted to, but I've tried to avoid it. I'd cling to him and shut my eyes. He has examined every inch of me, to the very pores of my skin, but I haven't known his body nearly as well as I know Kimura's. I haven't wanted to. I suspected it would only make me detest him all the more. It gave me a queer feeling to think I've been sleeping with such a miserable creature. And he called *me* bow-legged!

Dr. Kodama spread my husband's legs about half a yard apart. Then, with the chopstick, he rubbed both sides of the scrotum, just as he'd rubbed the soles of the feet. (Later he explained that he was testing the reflexes of the suspensory muscles.) He rubbed one side and then the other, several times each. The right testicle made a slow up-and-down motion, like the squirming of a live abalone, but the left one didn't seem to move. (Toshiko and I tried to look away. Finally Toshiko left the room.) Next he took his temperature and measured his blood pressure. The temperature was normal. Blood pressure: 190+. Apparently it had dropped a bit as a result of the hemorrhage.

For over an hour and a half Dr. Kodama stayed at the bedside to see how his patient was getting along. During that time he drew one hundred grams of blood from a vein in his arm and gave him an injection of Neophyrin, vitamins B-1 and K, and a fifty-per-cent glucose concentrate.

"I'll call again in the afternoon," he said, "but it would be a good idea to have Dr. Noma look at him." That was something I'd intended to do anyway.

I asked if I should inform the relatives.

"I think you can afford to wait a little," he told me.

THE KEY

Dr. Kodama left at about four a.m. At the door, I asked him to send us a nurse as soon as possible.

At seven Baya came, and Toshiko went home to Sekidencho. She said she'd be back in the afternoon.

As soon as Toshiko was gone I called Kimura. I told him what had happened to my husband, and added that for the present he'd probably better not come over. He was quite disturbed, and said he wanted to stop in to see him for a moment, at least. But I explained that it might upset him —in spite of his paralysis and loss of speech, he still seemed to be partly conscious. "Then let me come to the front door," Kimura said. "I won't go to his room."

Around nine o'clock my husband began to snore. It's an old habit of his, but today it was different, really dreadful. He seemed to have lapsed into a coma. I telephoned Kimura again to say there'd be no harm in looking in on him, if he continued like this.

Dr. Kodama phoned at eleven. "I've been in touch with Dr. Noma," he told me. "We'll be over to see the patient at two o'clock."

At twelve thirty Kimura arrived, between

138

classes. He went to the sickroom and sat at the bedside for about half an hour. I stayed too; Kimura sat in the chair, and I on the other bed (my husband was in mine). We exchanged a few words now and then. Meanwhile the snoring got louder and louder, until it seemed quite thunderous. Suddenly I wondered if it was genuine. I could see that Kimura noticed my misgivings, and even shared them, but of course neither of us said anything about it. At one o'clock he left. The nurse arrived—a pretty girl in her early twenties named Koike. Toshiko came too. At last I was free, so I went to the kitchen to eat. It was my first meal since yesterday.

At two Dr. Noma arrived, along with Dr. Kodama. Since morning my husband had developed a 100.8° fever. Dr. Noma seemed to be in general agreement with Dr. Kodama. He tested Babinski's reflex again, but not the other one (apparently it's called the scrotal reflex). He didn't think it wise to deplete the blood very much. And he gave Dr. Kodama some further advice, in technical language.

After the doctors had gone, the massage therapist turned up for another session. Toshiko sent him away, with a sarcastic remark about how his treatments had helped her father. That was because Dr. Kodama said, earlier, that the long, drastic massage might have brought on my husband's stroke. (I suppose he was trying to console me.) Baya apologized profusely. Introducing that man was a terrible thing to have done, she said.

A little after three Toshiko suggested I lie down for a while, and I decided it was a good chance to get some sleep. The bedroom was occupied, of course, and there was a good deal of coming and going through the sitting room. Toshiko's room was free, but she doesn't like anyone else to use it; she keeps her closet doors, bookcases, and desk drawers all locked tight. I've hardly ever set foot in it. So I came upstairs to the study, spread the bedding out on the floor, and lay down to sleep. I suppose the nurse and I will be taking turns here. But I had to admit that I was in no mood for sleep. I wanted to catch up with my diary—which I'd smuggled along with me, making sure not to let Toshiko notice. After spending an hour and a half at it, I finished the entry for the seventeenth. Then I hid the diary behind the bookshelf and went downstairs, as if I had just awakened. It wasn't quite five o'clock.

My husband had emerged from his coma.

Now and then he opened his eyes a little and glanced around. I was told he'd been doing it for about twenty minutes. The coma had lasted since nine a.m., over seven hours. Miss Koike said she'd heard it was dangerous if it lasted twenty-four hours, and so he was getting along well. But the left side of his body still seemed to be paralyzed.

About five thirty he began mumbling, as if he wanted to talk. I couldn't understand what he was trying to say, but he didn't sound quite as inarticulate as before. He moved his right hand slightly, pointing to the lower part of his abdomen. I guessed that he wanted to urinate, and gave him the bedpan. But he didn't pass anything. He seemed to be terribly irritated. He nodded when I asked if he wanted to make water, so I tried again—and again nothing came out. It must have been painful, since his urine had been collecting for such a long time. I decided that his bladder was paralyzed. After calling Dr. Kodama to get instructions, I sent out for a catheter, which Miss Koike used to draw off the urine. I could see that there was a great deal.

At seven we gave him a little milk and fruit juice through a straw.

At ten thirty Baya went home. She said she couldn't stay overnight, because of her family. Toshiko asked if I needed her for anything. I knew that she was implying: "There's no reason why I shouldn't stay, except that it might be inconvenient for you." I told her she could do as she pleased; there was no special danger; the patient seemed to be holding his own. I could let her know if he took a turn for the worse. "Yes, I suppose so," she said, and at eleven she left for Sekidencho.

He seemed to be dozing, not sleeping very soundly.

APRIL 19

••

At midnight Miss Koike and I were sitting quietly together in the sickroom. We had turned the lamp away from my husband, and were passing the time reading newspapers and magazines. I urged her to go and rest for a little, but she didn't want to. About five o'clock, when it was already getting light, she finally went upstairs.

The sun began filtering in through the shutters, and it seemed to disturb my husband's sleep. Suddenly I noticed that his eyes were open, staring in my direction. He seemed to be looking for me—I wonder if he really couldn't see me as I sat there beside him. He was trying to say something. All I recognized—or thought I recognized—was a single word. Maybe it was just my imagination, but he seemed to be saying "Ki—mu—ra." The rest was only a kind of gurgling sound, but that much seemed unmistakable. Maybe he'd have said the rest of it more clearly, too, if it hadn't been quite so embarrassing. After repeating it two or three times he stopped, and shut his eyes.

At seven Baya arrived, and then Toshiko. An hour later Miss Koike came downstairs.

At eight thirty we gave him his breakfast: a bowl of thin rice gruel, an egg yolk, apple juice. I spooned it up for him. He seemed to want me, rather than Miss Koike, to take care of him.

A little after ten o'clock he wanted to urinate. I tried to get him to use the bedpan, but nothing came out. When Miss Koike tried to draw off the urine, he objected, and made a gesture as if to say: "Take that thing away!" All we could do was give him the bedpan again. After ten minutes there were still no results. He seemed terribly annoyed. Miss Koike brought out the catheter again, and talked to him as if she were trying to reason with a child. "You may not like this, but you'll feel a lot better afterward. Come on, you'll let me use it, won't you? You'll feel better right away."

He was trying to tell us something, trying to indicate it with his hands. All three of us—Miss Koike, Toshiko, and I—kept asking him what he wanted. We gathered that he was talking to me, and saying: "If the catheter has to be used, you use it. Have Toshiko and the nurse go away." At last Toshiko and I persuaded him that the nurse was the only one who could do it properly.

At noon we gave him his lunch. It was about what he'd had this morning, but his appetite seemed fairly good.

At twelve thirty Kimura arrived. Today I only talked to him at the door. I told him that my husband was out of his coma, that he seemed to be gradually improving, that he'd mumbled something that sounded to me like "Kimura."

One p.m. A visit from Dr. Kodama. He said the patient was making satisfactory progress. We still had to be very careful, but if his recovery continued at this rate, everything would be fine. Systolic blood pressure 165, diastolic, 110. Temperature down to 99°. Again today he tested Babinski's reflex and the scrotal reflex. During the latter I wondered uneasily whether my husband would put up with it. But he did, staring off into space with glazed, expressionless eyes. Dr. Kodama also gave him an intravenous injection of dextrose, Neophyrin, and vitamins.

I've tried as far as possible not to let anyone know about his stroke, but the news has leaked out at school. This afternoon there were a number of telephone calls and visitors; people have begun sending fruit, flowers, and other such things, too. Madame Okada came over, and was all the more sympathetic when she learned that it was the same illness as her husband's. She left us some lilacs from her garden. Toshiko filled a vase with them, brought it into the sickroom, and placed it on a bedside table. "Papa, these are from Madame Okada's garden," she told him. We'd also received some mandarin oranges, which he likes. I squeezed them in the mixer and gave him the juice.

At three I left everything to Toshiko and Miss Koike, and came upstairs. After writing in my diary, I tried to get some sleep. Naturally I was very tired by then, and I slept soundly for about three hours.

Tonight Toshiko went home at eight, soon after dinner. Baya left at nine thirty.

APRIL 20

• •

One a.m. Miss Koike went upstairs to sleep, and I stayed alone with my husband. He had been dozing since early evening. About ten minutes after she left, though, I began to think he might really be awake. He was lying in the shadow, but I could hear him stirring and mumbling. Stealthily I peered over at him, and saw that, just as I'd imagined, he was lying there with his eyes open. He was looking in my direction, but beyond me. Those lilacs Toshiko had brought in—his eyes seemed fixed on them. The lamp was shaded so that it lighted up only a small part of the room; within that little pool of lamplight, barely enough for reading a newspaper, the lilacs were dimly glowing. He seemed to be staring blankly at their

146

pale silhouette, as if he were lost in thought. It bothered me, somehow. Yesterday, when Toshiko told him they were from Madame Okada's garden, it occurred to me—though I can't say what prompted her to do it—that she needn't have mentioned it just then. I suppose he heard what she said. Even if he didn't, those flowers must have reminded him of the lilac bush in the garden at Sekidencho. And then he must have thought of Toshiko's cottage, and of all that had happened there at night.

It may have been only my imagination, but as I looked into his eyes I thought that fantasies of that sort were drifting in their vacant depths. Hurriedly I turned the lamp away from the flowers.

Seven a.m. I took the lilac vase out of the bedroom, replacing it with some roses in a glass bowl.

One p.m. A visit from Dr. Kodama. Temperature down to 98.2°. Blood pressure rising again: Systolic, 185, diastolic, 140. To correct it, an injection of Neohypotonine. Again today Dr. Kodama performed that scrotal-reflex test. I went to the door with him, and stepped outside to consult him about a few things. I told him that the paralysis of the bladder continued, so that Miss Koike had had to use the catheter again this morning; that my husband was annoyed every time she did it; that the slightest thing seemed to get on his nerves, but what especially irritated him was that his hands and legs and mouth didn't work the way he wanted them to.

Dr. Kodama says we should give him Luminal to calm him down and make sure he sleeps.

Today Toshiko didn't turn up until five p.m. About ten o'clock I began to hear my husband snoring—not that abnormal snoring of the day before yesterday, but the way he usually sounds when he's asleep. Apparently the injection of Luminal had already taken effect. Toshiko watched his face a moment, and remarked that he seemed to be having a good rest. She left soon after. Baya left too. I sent Miss Koike up to bed.

Toward eleven o'clock the phone rang. It was Kimura. "I'm sorry to bother you at this hour," he said. (Had Toshiko told him I'd be alone now?) He asked how my husband was getting along. I told him, and mentioned that he was sound asleep, under sedation.

148

"Could I just look in for a moment?" he asked. Look in at whom? I wondered.

"Yes, if you'll wait in the garden till I come out the back way," I answered, very softly, my mouth close to the telephone. "You mustn't ring the doorbell. If I don't come out, you'll know it isn't convenient, so please go on home."

Fifteen minutes later I heard a faint sound of footsteps in the garden. My husband's noisy breathing went on as steadily as ever. I brought Kimura in through the back door, and we talked for half an hour in the maid's room.

When I returned to my husband, he was still snoring peacefully.

APRIL 21

• •

One p.m. A visit from Dr. Kodama. Systolic blood pressure 180, diastolic, 136. It's gone down a little, but he won't be out of danger until the diastolic is in the 170's with a difference of at least fifty between the two readings. But his temperature is finally back to normal. This morning he managed to pass urine, using the bedpan. His appetite is good; he eats anything I give him, though for the present he's on a soft diet.

At two o'clock I left Miss Koike in charge and went up to bed. After writing in my diary, I slept till five. When I came down, Toshiko had arrived. At five thirty, half an hour before dinner, we gave him another injection of Luminal. Dr. Kodama advised us to give it to him regularly at this time, since it takes effect only after four or five hours. But he warned Miss Koike not to say that it was a sedative: she should let him think it was something to lower his blood pressure.

At six o'clock, when he saw the dinner tray, my husband started mumbling. Whatever he was saying, he repeated it two or three times. I spooned up some of the rice gruel for him, but he said it again, as if to hold back my hand. I thought perhaps he didn't like having me serve him, so Toshiko, and then Miss Koike, tried instead. But that wasn't it. Meanwhile, I'd gradually begun to understand him. Fantastic as it seemed, he was saying "Be-e-e-f st-e-eak." And as he said it he glanced quickly at me, with a look of appeal, then shut his eyes again. I could guess what was in his mind, but Miss Koike—and Toshiko?—probably couldn't. I shook my head at him, discreetly, to hint that he would have to wait, that he mustn't even think of such a thing now. I wonder if he understood. In any case, he let it go at that, and opened his mouth meekly to sip the gruel that I held out to him.

At eight o'clock Toshiko left; at nine, Baya. At ten he fell sound asleep and began snoring. I sent Miss Koike upstairs.

At eleven I heard footsteps in the garden. I brought him in the back way, to the maid's room. He left at twelve. The snoring continued.

APRIL 22
••

Not much change in his condition. His blood pressure was a little higher again. He sleeps well enough under sedation, but during the day his mind is clouded, and he's often irritable. Although Dr. Kodama says he needs at least twelve hours of sound sleep, he probably doesn't get more than six or seven. The rest of the time he seems to be merely dozing. On the whole, it's been my experience that he's not really asleep unless he's snoring—but now there are times when even his snoring sounds suspicious. Tomorrow, with the doctor's permission, we're going to begin giving him Luminal twice a day: once in the morning and once in the afternoon.

Toshiko and Baya left at their usual times. At ten o'clock the snoring began. At eleven I heard footsteps in the garden.

APRIL 23

• •

It's been almost a week since he had his stroke. At nine a.m., when Miss Koike was taking the breakfast tray back to the kitchen, he saw that we were alone, and began trying to talk. "Di-a-ry, di-a-ry," he was saying. Compared with yesterday's "be-e-e-f st-e-e-ak," it sounded quite distinct. Again he repeated the word "diary." Evidently it was weighing on his mind.

"Do you want to write in your diary?" I asked. "But that's still too much for you!"

He shook his head.

"No?" I said. "It's not your diary, then?"

"*Your* diary . . ." he answered.

"Mine?" I exclaimed.

He nodded, and said: "You . . . what are you doing . . . about your diary?"

I pretended to be annoyed. "You know very well I've never kept a diary."

He smiled weakly, and nodded as if to say: "Yes, of course! I understand." It was the first time he had smiled for me, even faintly, but his smile was a rather perplexing one.

Miss Koike had her own breakfast in the sitting room; she came back at about ten o'clock. Then, without a word, she began getting ready to inject the Luminal into his arm.

"What's this?" he asked suspiciously. He'd never had an injection at this time in the morning.

"Your blood pressure is still a little high," she told him. "I'm giving you something to bring it down."

One p.m. Visit from Dr. Kodama. Around two thirty, noticing that my husband had begun to snore, I went upstairs. When I came down at five the snoring had already stopped. According to Miss Koike, he slept less than an hour; after that he seemed to be dozing. Apparently he still can't rest very well in the daytime, even with a sedative. After dinner we gave him the second injection.

At eleven sharp I heard footsteps in the garden.

APRIL 24

• •

This was the first Sunday after his stroke. We had two or three callers, but I didn't ask them in. Dr. Kodama didn't come to see him. No change in his condition.

Toshiko arrived about two o'clock, a good deal earlier than usual. She's been coming late in the afternoon, and staying only a few hours. Today, as she stood there beside her father, who was fast asleep, she said: "I thought you might have a lot of visitors." She was watching my face.

When I didn't answer, she went on: "Mama, don't you have any shopping to do? Why don't you go out for a little fresh air, now that it's Sunday?"

Was that really her own idea? I wondered. Maybe he asked her to suggest it. Of course he could easily have said something to me. Did he prefer to have Toshiko do it for him, or was she simply acting on her own suspicions? . . . Suddenly I could see him at our Osaka hotel, eagerly awaiting me, at that very moment. Suppose he actually *was* there—but then I checked myself. After all, it seemed most unlikely. Yet the notion kept coming back to me. Clearly, though, I didn't have time to go to Osaka. I couldn't possibly be away that long, at least not until next Sunday.

However, there was something else on my mind, so I told Toshiko I'd go to pick up a few things at the Nishiki market. "I'll be back in an hour," I said. It was three o'clock when I left the house.

I found a taxi and hurried down to Nishiki Street. First, to justify the trip, I bought wheat-gluten cakes, toasted bean curd, and some vegetables. After that I walked up Teramachi as far as Sanjo, and stopped in at the stationer's for ten large sheets of rice paper and a sheet of cardboard. I had them all cut to the size of my diary and carefully wrapped; then I put them in my shopping bag, under the vegetables. I went over to Kawaramachi Street for a taxi—but I mustn't forget to mention that I telephoned him from the market.

"No, I wasn't planning to go out at all today," he told me. He said it hesitantly, as if he thought I might be suggesting we meet. But we only talked for a few minutes.

I got home a little after four (I'd been gone just over an hour), hid the package of rice paper behind the umbrella rack, and took the shopping bag out to Baya in the kitchen. My husband still seemed to be asleep, though he wasn't snoring.

What had bothered me was his question about my diary. Why had he come out with that? Had he forgotten, in his confused mental state, that he wasn't supposed to know about it? Or was he saying: "I don't see any more need to pretend"? And when I tried to wriggle out of it by telling him I've never kept one, did that odd smile of his mean "Stop playing innocent"? Anyway, he obviously wanted to know if I'd kept up my diary. Next he will want to see it. Since he can no longer read it behind my back, he's begun to hint that he'd like my permission. I have to be ready for the time when he asks me openly.

As far as the entries up to the sixteenth of this month are concerned, I'm willing to show them to him whenever he likes. But he must never know that it doesn't stop there. "You've been reading my diary in secret," I'll tell him, "so there's no use hiding it any more. Look at it all you want, though it's hardly worth showing to you. As you'll see, it ends on the sixteenth. Since then, I've been far too busy to have time for keeping up a diary—not that I've done anything worth writing about."

But I'll have to prove it by showing him there are only empty pages after the sixteenth. With my new rice paper, I can divide the book at that point, add the proper number of blank sheets, and rebind it in two volumes.

I'd missed my afternoon nap, so I went upstairs to rest for about an hour. When I came down at half-past six I brought along the diary and put it in the drawer of the sitting-room cabinet. Toshiko left after dinner, at eight o'clock. At ten I had Miss Koike go upstairs. At eleven I heard footsteps in the garden.

APRIL 25

• •

At midnight I saw him out and fastened the kitchen door. Then I stayed in the bedroom about an hour, listening intently. As soon as I'd satisfied myself that my husband was asleep, I went to the sitting room and got to work rebinding my diary. When I finished I put the part with the old entries back in the cabinet drawer, and took the other upstairs and hid it behind the bookshelves. It was after two o'clock when I returned to the bedroom. He was still fast asleep.

One p.m. Visit from Dr. Kodama. No particular change. Lately his blood pressure has been fluctuating in the 180's. Dr. Kodama frowned, and said he wished it would go down a little further. As usual, my husband couldn't seem to sleep very well during the day.

At eleven I heard footsteps in the garden.

APRIL 28

• •

At eleven, footsteps in the garden . . .

APRIL 29

• •

At eleven, footsteps in the garden . . .

APRIL 30

• •

One p.m. Visit from Dr. Kodama. He says Dr.
Noma ought to have another look at the patient
early next week.

MAY 1

• •

This was the second Sunday after his stroke.
Again Toshiko arrived early, as I'd expected. She
listened to make sure her father was asleep, then,
in a low voice, urged me to go out shopping and
get a little air.

"Should I?" I said, hesitating.

"Papa's all right," she assured me. "He's just

159

THE KEY

fallen asleep. Go ahead, Mama, and stop in at Sekidencho on your way home. We've got the bath heated."

I guessed that there was something behind it. "Well, then, just for an hour or two," I said. It was about three o'clock when I left the house.

I went straight to Sekidencho. Kimura was there alone. He said Toshiko had phoned to ask him to come over for two or three hours, while she went to visit her father. She told him she'd promised to look after the house for Madame Okada, who was spending the day in Wakayama. The bath was stone cold.

For the first time in weeks we were able to have a few leisurely hours together. Yet somehow we felt restless; we couldn't seem to relax. . . . At five I left him there and hurried out to do my shopping at a nearby market. I was afraid my husband might have awakened.

"You're back early," Toshiko said. When I asked how Papa had been, she told me he'd slept amazingly well—more than three hours already. Sure enough, he was snoring loudly.

"Your daughter took care of the patient while I went for a bath," Miss Koike said, her pink, shiny face glowing as if she had just stepped out of the tub. So she had gone to the bathhouse! I couldn't help thinking Toshiko had seen to it. Of course it was Miss Koike's turn to go; we've only heated our own bath two or three times since my husband has been sick, and Baya, Miss Koike, and I have been going to the public bathhouse every other day or so, in the afternoon. Toshiko must have known that when she sent me out. It was careless of me not to have thought of it myself. I suppose I would have—and would have remembered that Miss Koike takes almost an hour at her bath—except that when Toshiko mentioned Sekidencho it made my heart leap, made me forget all about being cautious.

Now I've done it! I thought, as I left them to go upstairs for my nap.

I took the diary from its hiding place behind the bookshelves and examined it very carefully. I should have sealed it with Scotch tape, perhaps, but I hadn't dreamed of being *that* cautious. And so there was no way for me to find out— but I told myself I was only imagining things. I had let my suspicions carry me too far. How could anyone know I'd taken my diary apart and hidden this section of it upstairs? Looking at the matter that way gave me a sense of relief.

But at eight, when Toshiko left for Seki-dencho, I started worrying again. I went to the kitchen and asked Baya if anyone had gone up to the study this afternoon. She surprised me by saying that Toshiko had. Apparently Miss Koike left about fifteen minutes after I did; then Toshiko went upstairs. She came down in a few minutes and went back to the bedroom. "She seemed to be talking to the master about something," Baya said.

"I thought he was asleep," I said.

"He woke up suddenly," she told me, and added that Toshiko went upstairs again later, but stayed only a moment. Then Miss Koike came back from the bathhouse.

"But he was snoring when I got home," I objected.

"Not while you were gone," she said. "He fell asleep just before you came in."

I began to realize that my fears were not quite so groundless as I had supposed. Perhaps I should try to set down what Toshiko must have done today. At three o'clock, after managing to get rid of me, she sent Miss Koike off to the bathhouse. Then—whether or not my husband put her up to it—she hunted out my diary in the sitting-room cabinet and brought it to him. He noticed that it stops on April sixteenth, and told her there should be another book hidden somewhere—that's the one he wanted to see! Next she rummaged through the bookshelves in his study, found it, and brought it down to show him. Maybe she read it aloud to him. After that she took it upstairs and put it back in its hiding place. Miss Koike returned. Again he pretended to be fast asleep. At five I came home.

But, supposing I've guessed right, how shall I protect my diary now? I can't bring myself to give it up just because of a single blunder. Still, I've got to make sure it won't happen again. From now on I'll stop writing upstairs during my nap time. Late at night, after my husband and Miss Koike are both asleep, I'll make a new entry, and then hide the book away in some really safe place.

JUNE 9

• •

For a long time I've neglected my diary. I haven't touched it since May first—the day before my

163

husband was carried off by another stroke. That is partly because his sudden death burdened me with all sorts of family duties; partly, too, it's because I lost the desire—perhaps I should say incentive—to go ahead with it. My reason for "losing incentive" remains unchanged, and so this may be my final entry. At least, I haven't yet decided to go on.

I do feel that a diary I've succeeded in keeping up for four whole months deserves to be brought to a conclusion, rather than simply dropped. But I'm not just being tidy. I think it will be worth my while, at this point, to look back once again at the conflict in our sexual life, and try to recall its various phases. If I compare his diary with my own I ought to be able to understand what really happened. Then there were a number of things I hesitated to put in writing while he was alive. I'd like to add them as a kind of postscript, to bring this account to a close.

As I've said, my husband died suddenly. I don't know the precise time, but it was on May second—probably around three a.m. His nurse, Miss Koike, was sleeping upstairs, and Toshiko had gone back to Sekidencho. I was the only one left taking care of him. At two, since he was snoring peacefully, I slipped out to the sitting room, where I began making an entry in my diary. Until then—from the time he fell ill, that is— I'd done my writing during the afternoon. I'd go upstairs for my nap, and steal the chance to jot down what had happened the day before. But on Sunday, May first, I got the impression that this part of my diary, which I'd carefully hidden, was being read by Toshiko and my husband. I decided to change my habits, do all my writing late at night, and find a new hiding place. However, since I couldn't think of a good one, I left the diary in its usual place and went downstairs. That night, as soon as Toshiko and Baya were gone, I took it out again and tucked it away in the folds of my kimono. Soon afterward Miss Koike went to bed. I was worried because I still hadn't hit on a safe place for it. Of course I had the whole night to think of one; if necessary, I could even stuff it between the loose ceiling boards in the sitting-room closet.

At two a.m. on May second, then, I went to the sitting room, took out the diary I'd been carrying, and began writing. Some time later I realized with a start that my husband's breathing, so noisy until a few moments ago, had become

165

THE KEY

inaudible. There was only a thin wall between us, but I'd been so absorbed that I hadn't noticed the silence. I became aware of it just as I finished writing these words: "Late at night, after my husband and Miss Koike are both asleep, I'll make a new entry, and then hide the book away in some really safe place."

I put down my brush and listened, my ears cocked toward the bedroom. But I couldn't hear anything, so I got up, leaving my diary on the table, and went to look at him. He was lying on his back, his face turned straight up. (That was the way he usually slept, with his gray, naked face —he never wore glasses after his stroke—in full view. I could scarcely avoid looking at it.) He seemed to be sleeping quietly. It was hard to tell, though, since a cloth had been draped over the lamp shade, and his head lay in the shadow.

I sat down for a moment and watched him, there in the gloom. But he seemed strangely quiet, so quiet that I uncovered the lamp and let the bare light strike his face. Then I saw that his eyes were half open, fixed in a rigid, slantwise stare. He's dead, I thought; and when I went over to touch his hand, it was cold. The clock said seven minutes past three. And so I can only be sure that he died sometime between two and three a.m. on May second. He must have died in his sleep, without pain. For a few moments, like a coward peering into the depths of an abyss, I held my breath and looked into that gray, naked face. Memories of our honeymoon night came flooding into my mind. Then I hastily covered the lamp again.

The next day both Dr. Noma and Dr. Kodama told me they hadn't expected him to have another stroke so soon. Till about ten years ago, they said, most patients suffered their second attack of cerebral anemia after two or three— at the longest, seven or eight—more years, and the second one was usually fatal. Now, however, thanks to the progress of medicine, that was no longer true. Some people had one or two strokes and then recovered; some even survived three or four. With my husband, there was clearly danger of a relapse, because, unlike most educated men, he tended to ignore his doctor's advice. Still, they hadn't thought it would come so soon. He wasn't sixty yet; once he had regained his health, no matter how slowly, he ought to have been active for several more years—over ten years, if all went well. It was really quite unexpected . . . or so they said.

Of course I can't tell if they were being honest with me, but maybe they were. Doctors are never very accurate about predicting how long a man will live. As for myself, I felt it had happened more or less as I'd expected. It didn't come as a shock to me. I'm often wrong in my intuitions, more often than not, perhaps; but this time I guessed right. So did Toshiko, I imagine.

Now I want to reread our diaries and compare them, tracing the steps by which we came to this final parting. To be sure, he told me he began keeping a diary years ago, before we were married; maybe I ought to start there in order to study our relations thoroughly. But I'm not the kind of person for such a research project. I know there are dozens of diaries piled up in the closet in his study, so high you can't reach them without a ladder; but I don't have the patience to wade through those dusty old books. As he said himself, he used to be careful not to mention anything about our sexual life. It was in January that he began writing about it freely—almost exclusively—and that I began to contend with him by keeping a diary of my own. By comparing entries from that time on (and filling in what we left out), I ought to be able to see how we loved, how we indulged our passions, how we deceived and ensnared each other, until one of us was destroyed. I don't think there'll be any need for me to go further back.

In his New Year's Day entry he says that I am "furtive, fond of secrets, constantly holding back and pretending ignorance." That is perfectly true. On the whole, he was far more honest than I was—I have to admit that his diary has very few falsehoods in it. It has a few, though. For instance, he says: "It seems unlikely that she would dip into her husband's private writings. . . . I have decided not to worry about that any more." I saw at once that his real motive was just as he later admitted: "Secretly, I hoped that she was reading it."

The fact that he purposely dropped the key (on the morning of January fourth) proves that he wanted me to read his diary. Really, he needn't have bothered to tempt me. On January fourth I said: "I shall never read it. I haven't the faintest desire to penetrate his psychology, beyond the limits I've set for myself. I don't like to let others know what is in my own mind, and I don't care to pry into theirs." But that wasn't true— except when I said: "I don't like to let others know what is in my own mind." Soon after our marriage I got into the habit of glancing over his secret notebooks. Of course I'd "known about his diary for a long time." It's nonsense to say "I'd never dream of touching it."

In the past, though, he concentrated on what were, to me, dry-as-dust academic matters. And so I merely leafed through the pages now and then, for the mild satisfaction of reading something of my husband's behind his back. But ever since he "decided not to worry about that," I've naturally been drawn to his diary. As early as January second, while he was out on a walk, I discovered how it had changed. Still, it wasn't just because I like to "pretend ignorance" that I kept on being so secretive about it. I could tell that that was what he wanted me to do.

I think he was being quite sincere when he called me his "beloved wife." I haven't the slightest doubt of his love. In the beginning I myself felt a passionate love for him. I can't deny that "I accepted a man who was utterly wrong for me," nor that "sometimes the very sight of him made me queasy." But that doesn't mean I didn't love him. Having had an "old-fashioned Kyoto upbringing," I "married him because my parents wanted me to, and I thought marriage was supposed to be like this." I had no choice but to love him. He was right to say I set great store by my "antiquated morality." Whenever I began to be sickened by him, I felt ashamed of myself. I thought I was behaving inexcusably toward my dead parents, as well as toward him; the more I loathed him, the more I tried to love him. And I succeeded. Driven by sexual hunger, I could do nothing less.

At the time, my only regret was that he didn't fully satisfy me. Instead of accusing him of weakness, though, I felt ashamed of my own lustful appetite. I was sorry about his declining vigor, and, far from blaming him, tried to be all the more devoted. But since January I've had to look at him in a new light. It's still not clear to me why he decided he would "begin writing freely." He said it was "out of frustration at never having a chance to talk to her about our sexual problems . . . because of her extreme reticence —her 'refinement,' her 'femininity,' her so-called

modesty." He wanted to sweep away all that—
but wasn't there another reason, too? I think
there was, though I can't find anything clearcut
about it in his diary. Maybe even he didn't understand his real motive.

Anyway, I learned that my "physical endowment for it is equaled by very few women."
But then he said: "Perhaps I shouldn't mention
this. At the very least, it may put me at a disadvantage." Why did he decide to run the risk? He
said that the mere thought of it made him jealous,
that he worried about what might happen "if another man knew of it." Yet he deliberately mentioned it in his diary.

I took that to mean he hoped I would give
him cause to doubt me. And, later on, he wrote:
"I secretly enjoyed being jealous. Such feelings
have always given me an erotic stimulus; in a
sense, they're both necessary and pleasurable to
me" (January thirteenth). But I had already
gathered that from his New Year's Day entry.

• •

On January eighth I wrote: "I violently dislike
my husband, and just as violently love him. No
matter how much he disgusts me I shall never give
myself to another man."

For twenty years I'd felt obliged to suppress
my dissatisfaction with my husband. That is why,
in spite of a strict Kyoto upbringing, I allowed
myself to write unpleasant things about him.
Above all, though, I'd begun to understand that
making him jealous was the way to make him
happy—and that that was the duty of a "model
wife." Still, I'd only said: "I violently dislike my
husband"—and then added feebly: "I shall never
give myself to another man." Maybe I already
loved Kimura without realizing it. All I did—
fearfully, and in a roundabout way at that—was
to drop a disturbing hint. And I did it reluctantly,
from a sense of duty.

But my feelings changed when I read his
entry of the thirteenth: "Stimulated by jealousy,
I succeeded in satisfying Ikuko. . . . I want her
to make me insanely jealous. . . . Not that

there shouldn't be an element of danger—the more the better."

My thoughts turned suddenly to Kimura. On the seventh my husband had written: "Although Ikuko may believe that she is merely acting as a chaperone, I think she finds Kimura extremely attractive." But that had only repelled me, made me think that, no matter what he said, I couldn't possibly be so immoral. When it came to being told "the more the better," I had a change of heart. I'm not sure whether he said it because he realized—before I did—that I liked Kimura, or whether it was what he said that began to stir my interest. Even after I knew I was drifting into love with Kimura, I went on deceiving myself, as long as I could, that I was doing it reluctantly, for the sake of my husband. Yes, I was already drifting into love, but I told myself I was only trying to show a little interest in another man.

On the first night I fainted (January twenty-eighth, that is) I could no longer explain my feelings for Kimura that way; all I could do was try to conceal my suffering. I slept straight through to the morning of the thirtieth. He wrote: "Of course she may have been only shamming." I certainly wasn't shamming, though I can hardly

174

say I remained unconscious all that time. I suppose he was right in calling me half awake; but as to whether I was "really delirious" when I murmured Kimura's name, or whether "that was only a subterfuge," I'd say it was somewhere between the two. It's true I was "dreaming of making love with Kimura"; but just then I became vaguely—only vaguely—aware that I'd called his name. How shameful of me! I thought. Yet as much as it embarrassed me to have my husband hear such a thing, I *did* feel, too, that what had happened was for the best.

But the case was different on the following night (the thirtieth), even though he said: "She murmured Kimura's name again—was she having that same dream, that same delusion, just as she had had before?" That night I did it intentionally. I can't say I'd formed a definite purpose—maybe I was dreaming a little, after all—but that haziness helped to still my conscience. "Should I, perhaps, interpret it as a kind of ridicule?" he wondered. Maybe he was right. I was trying to tell him how I longed to be in Kimura's arms instead of his, and how I wished he would bring the two of us together. That is what I wanted him to understand.

On February fourteenth Kimura told my husband about the Polaroid camera. "But how did he guess that I would be pleased to learn about such a camera? That puzzles me." It puzzled me, too. I hadn't guessed that my husband wanted to take nude photographs of me. Even if I had, I couldn't have said so to Kimura. At that time I was being carried to bed by him, drunk, nearly every night; but I never had a private talk with him, much less tell him anything about our sexual life. The truth is I had no other relations with him—I didn't have the chance. Personally, I was inclined to suspect Toshiko. She's the only one who could have given him the hint.

On February ninth she asked permission to live alone, in Sekidencho, saying she wanted a quiet place to study. It wasn't hard to imagine that "a quiet place" meant somewhere away from her parents' bedroom. She must have been peering in night after night at that garishly lighted spectacle—what with the roaring of the stove, we couldn't have heard her footsteps. I suppose she saw my husband stripping me naked and doing all sorts of lewd things. And I suppose she told Kimura about it. Later my suspicions were more or less confirmed, but I'd already guessed as much

176

from my husband's diary of the fourteenth. Toshiko probably knew what was going on—and reported it to Kimura—even before I did.

But why did Kimura tell my husband about that special camera, as if to suggest photographing me in the nude? I haven't asked him yet, but perhaps he was trying to curry favor. Besides, he must have hoped to see the pictures someday. Probably that was his main reason. I suppose he expected my husband to turn from the Polaroid to the Zeiss Ikon, and to want him to do the developing.

On February nineteenth I wrote: "I cannot imagine what is in Toshiko's mind." That wasn't quite accurate. As I've said, I already felt sure she'd told Kimura what went on in our bedroom, and I realized, too, that she was in love with him. That's why she was "secretly hostile to me." It's true she worried about my health, and hated her father for "forcing me to satisfy his sexual demands." But when she saw him bringing Kimura and me together, and saw us indulging his strange whim, she began to hate me too. I suspected that very soon. Toshiko is wily, and knows that "though she's twenty years younger, she's actually not as attractive as I am in face or figure." Knowing, too, that Kimura was falling in love with me, she decided to act as go-between for us; then, at leisure, she could devise a scheme of her own. That much was clear to me. Yet even now I'm not sure how closely she and Kimura worked together. For instance, I don't think she moved to Sekidencho merely to get away from home: the fact that Kimura was living nearby must have had something to do with it. Was it his idea or hers? He said she made the ar-rangements ("I only followed her lead")—but I wonder if that was true. I'm afraid I still don't trust him.

At heart, I was as jealous of Toshiko as she was of me. But I tried not to let anyone notice it, nor to betray it in my diary. That was partly out of my natural secretiveness; even more, though, it was because I felt superior to her, and my pride was involved. Most of all, I was afraid my hus-band might think that I had reason to be jealous, that I suspected Kimura of being interested in her. My husband wrote: "If I were he, and had to say which of the two I found more attractive, I have no doubt that, despite her age, I would choose the mother." But he added: "I can't tell about him.

. . . He may be trying to improve his chances by ingratiating himself with Ikuko."

I didn't want to revive any notions of that kind. I wanted him to think of Kimura as completely infatuated with me, ready for any sacrifice on my account. Otherwise, his own jealousy would have been weakened.

JUNE 11

• •

On February twenty-seventh my husband said: "I was right, after all! Ikuko has been keeping a diary. . . . I got an inkling of it several days ago."

I'm sure he knew it long before, and was reading it behind my back. Of course I'd written: "I won't make the mistake of letting him suspect what I'm up to." But I was lying. I wanted him to read it. It's true I wanted to "talk to myself," too, but that wasn't really why I began keeping a diary. Being so secretive—using rice paper, sealing the book, and all that—was simply my natural way of going about it. Although he ridiculed me for it, he was just as bad. We knew we were reading each other's diaries, and still we set up all sorts of barriers, to make it as difficult and uncertain as possible. We preferred to be left in doubt. I didn't mind the trouble, since I was catering to both our tastes.

On April tenth I mentioned his illness for the first time. "I wonder if my husband's diary reveals anything about the state of his health. . . . For at least a month I've noticed that there's something wrong." Actually, he began writing about it on March tenth; but I think I noticed it even earlier, though I pretended I hadn't. I was afraid of worrying him, especially because he might feel he had to give up sexual intercourse. It's not that I wasn't concerned about his health, but the need to gratify my desire seemed far more urgent. Using Kimura to inflame his jealousy, I did all I could to make him forget his fear of death.

In April, though, my feelings slowly began to change. All through March I'd written that I was still stubbornly defending the "last line," and I did my best to convince him of it. In fact, it was on March twenty-fifth that I surrendered that last "paper-thin" defense. The next day I invented a harmless conversation with Kimura to put in my diary. I think it was early in April, around the fourth or the fifth, that I made a grave decision. Enticed into immorality, I'd been sinking lower and lower, but until then I'd deceived myself that it was only because I couldn't refuse what my husband wanted. I'd told myself I was behaving like a devoted wife, even from an old-fashioned moral point of view. But then I threw off the mask of self-deception, and frankly admitted I was in love with Kimura.

On April tenth I wrote: "He isn't the only one whose health is bad. I'm not much better off myself." Of course I wasn't at all sick—I had something else in mind. It's true that "when Toshiko was about ten, I started coughing up traces of blood, and the doctor warned me that I was showing symptoms of tuberculosis." But luckily "it turned out to be a mild case," and has never bothered me since. As for my statements that "one day in February, just as before, I coughed up a scarlet-flecked bit of phlegm containing a thread of blood," that "by afternoon I feel exhausted" and "my chest often aches quite severely," that this time I was afraid I might be

181

"gradually getting worse"—those were all down-right lies. I was trying to lure him into the shadow of death. I wanted him to think I was gambling my own life, and that he ought to be willing to risk his.

From then on my diary was written solely for that purpose. I didn't just write, though; sometimes I acted out my symptoms. I did everything I could to excite him, to keep him agitated, to drive his blood pressure higher and higher. (Even after his first stroke I kept on playing little tricks to make him jealous.) Long before, Kimura had hinted that my husband seemed on the verge of collapse. To me—and no doubt to Toshiko—his opinion meant more than any doctor's.

But why did I go so far as to scheme against my husband's life? Why did such an appalling thought come to me? Was it because anyone, no matter how gentle, would have been warped by the steady pressure of that degenerate, vicious mind of his? Maybe, deep down in me, I'd always been capable of it. It's something I'll have to think about. Yet I do feel, after all, that I can claim to have given him the kind of happiness he wanted.

I still have a good many suspicions about

Toshiko and Kimura. She said she found the Osaka hotel for us—through "a sophisticated friend" of hers—"because Mr. Kimura wondered if I knew of somewhere." Was that really all there was to it? She herself may have used that hotel with someone—may be using it even now.

According to Kimura's plan, he'll marry Toshiko when the mourning period is over. She'll make the sacrifice for the sake of appearances; and the three of us will live here together. That is what he tells me. . . .

A NOTE ABOUT THE AUTHOR

JUNICHIRO TANIZAKI was born in 1886 in the heart of downtown Tokyo, where his family owned a printing establishment. He studied Japanese literature at Tokyo Imperial University. His first published work, a one-act play, appeared in 1909 in a literary magazine he helped to found. His early novels suggest that his student days were ostentatiously bohemian, in the fashion of the day. At that time he was strongly influenced by Poe, Baudelaire, and Oscar Wilde.

He lived in the cosmopolitan Tokyo area until the earthquake of 1923, when he moved to the gentler and more cultured Kyoto-Osaka region, the scene of *The Makioka Sisters*. There he became absorbed in the Japanese past, and abandoned his superficial westernization. Japanese critics agree that this intellectual and emotional crisis changed him from merely a very good writer to a great one.

Tanizaki's most important novels were written after 1923; among them are *A Fool's Love* (1924), *Some Prefer Nettles* (1928), *Maelstrom* (1930), *Ashikari* (1932), a modern version of *The Tale of Genji* (1939–41), *The Makioka Sis-*

ters (1943–8), *Captain Shigemoto's Mother* (1949), and *The Key* (1956). By 1930 he had gained such fame that his "Complete Works" was published. He received the Imperial Prize in Literature in 1949.

A NOTE ABOUT THE TRANSLATOR

HOWARD HIBBETT took his doctorate at Harvard in Japanese literature and lived in Japan for three years. He has taught at the University of California, and is now Associate Professor of Japanese Literature at Harvard.

Library of Japanese Literature

THE MAKIOKA SISTERS *by Junichirō Tanizaki; translated by Edward G. Seidensticker*

MODERN JAPANESE LITERATURE: From 1868 to Present Day *compiled and edited by Donald Keene*

MODERN JAPANESE STORIES: An Anthology *edited by Ivan Morris, with translations by Edward Seidensticker, George Saito, Geoffrey Sargent, and Ivan Morris*

NIHONGI: Chronicles of Japan from the Earliest Times to A.D. 697 *translated from the original Chinese and Japanese by William George Aston*

OUT OF THE EAST: Reveries and Studies in New Japan *by Lafcadio Hearn*

A PERSONAL MATTER *by Kenzaburō Oë; translated by John Nathan*

THE PORNOGRAPHERS *by Akiyuki Nozaka; translated by Michael Gallagher*

RASHOMON AND OTHER STORIES *by Ryūnosuke Akutagawa; translated by Takashi Kojima*

THE ROMANCE OF THE MILKY WAY AND OTHER STUDIES AND STORIES *by Lafcadio Hearn*

THE RUINED MAP *by Kobo Abé; translated by E. Dale Saunders*

THE SAILOR WHO FELL FROM GRACE WITH THE SEA *by Yukio Mishima; translated by John Nathan*

SEVEN JAPANESE TALES *by Junichirō Tanizaki; translated by Howard Hibbett*

SHADOWINGS *by Lafcadio Hearn*

SHANKS' MARE: Being a Translation of the Tokaido Volumes of "Hizakurige," Japan's Great Comic Novel of Travel & Ribaldry *by Ikku Jippensha; translated by Thomas Satchell*

SNOW COUNTRY *by Yasunari Kawabata; translated, with an introduction, by Edward G. Seidensticker*

SOME PREFER NETTLES *by Junichirō Tanizaki; translated by Edward G. Seidensticker*

THE SOUND OF THE MOUNTAIN *by Yasunari Kawabata; translated by Edward G. Seidensticker*

THE SOUND OF WAVES *by Yukio Mishima; translated by Meredith Weatherby*

A STRANGE TALE FROM EAST OF THE RIVER AND OTHER STORIES *by Kafū Nagai; translated by Edward G. Seidensticker*

THE TALE OF GENJI *by Lady Murasaki; translated by Arthur Waley*

THE TALES OF ISE *translated from the classical Japanese by H. Jay Harris*

THE TEMPLE OF THE GOLDEN PAVILION *by Yukio Mishima; translated by Ivan Morris*

THE TEN FOOT SQUARE HUT AND TALES OF THE HEIKE: Being Two Thirteenth Century Japanese Classics, the "Hojoki" and selections from the "Heike Monogatari" *translated by A. L. Sadler*

THIRST FOR LOVE *by Yukio Mishima; translated by Alfred H. Marks*

CHARLES E. TUTTLE CO.: PUBLISHERS
Suido 1-chome, 2-6, Bunkyo-ku, Tokyo, Japan